MW00928127

Via Roma

Robert T. Norton

Library and Archives Canada Cataloguing in Publication

Norton, Robert, 1963 –

Via Roma / Robert T. Norton

ISBN 978-1-7753815-0-1

This is a work of fiction. Names, characters, places, and events
are the product of the author's imagination; or are actual places,
people and events used fictitiously. Any resemblance to any
unknown: persons, events, or locales is entirely coincidental.

Published by Plan B Press
a division of 2434346 Ontario Inc.

Table of Contents

For my Family and Friends -

You have made my Journey an exceptional one!

Pastore Nero

There is a park that I like to go to when I want to go local. I especially like to go there when I have had enough of the tourist hordes in the *Centro**.

The park is near the end of the *Linea A* of the *Metropolitana*, the southwest end. You exit at the *Guilio Agricola* stop, get topside and look for the big church. It is one of those architectural monstrosities from the late 60's.

On my way to the park, about two blocks before the church, I usually stop at this place on the south side of *Pza. Aurleno Celio Sabino*. I can't remember the name of it. I was never really good with names, places or people. Anyhow, they have decent coffee, and great pastries and lunch bites. I can't help feeling like a tourist whenever I drop in there.

Today I really needed to be in the park. Of course, I could have simply gone to *Villa Borghese* and lost myself at its middle, as I have done many times. Yet, that did not seem like enough of an escape. Today I needed that long *Metropolitana* ride out to the suburbs. I can't explain exactly why I needed this, and certainly not in a way that might satisfy your curiosity.

The ride was a typical off-peak one. Our car had a mere sprinkling of riders who were either very late for work, or perhaps their time was

---

* See Glossary P. 191

simply their own. If I recall correctly, it was at *Manzoni* station where this shiny skulled guy joined our car. He was a stale-dated hipster caricature with over-sized D & G sunglasses perched on his shaved dome, lots of gold chains and rings, skin-tight Versace t-shirt, and factory torn jeans.

He was barking into his cellphone non-stop; completely oblivious to the fact that he was subjecting other people to his one-dimensional half conversation. This vulgar exhibition of self-absorbed ignorance was really grating on my nerves.

I gazed up at the route map and counted off eight more stops to go before I could escape. I prayed that he would either get off at the next stop, or else end his call. I never pray for myself, only for others and rarely even at that.

Then a thought struck me. This guy was probably a hand-talker. Sure enough when I looked over at him his left hand was flying solo, flailing about like a kite in a heavy wind. His right hand was stationary, anchoring the phone to his ear. The more I watched, the more absurd it became to me.

I became convulsed with laughter. The hand-talker spun around and met my gaze. He immediately understood that I was laughing at him, though I am certain he did not know why I was. In response he glared at me and then quickly turned away. Only seconds later he ended his call and put his phone away. There were no more calls, and he never looked back in my direction.

A few stops later, I lost count - maybe five - the train reached *Guilo Agricola* station. As I disembarked, I never would have guessed that the hipster hand-talker and I would meet again only a couple of hours from now. My thoughts were comfortably elsewhere in that moment.

After so many visits you would think I would know which one of the four exits to take to end up on the correct side of *via Tuscolana* so that I could avoid the traffic lights. The truth is that I still do not.

It has become a game for me now. On the days when I choose the right exit I am overly impressed with myself. The times that I choose the wrong one, I chide my incompetent memory and promise myself that I will get it right on my next visit. To date, that promise has not been kept with any measure of consistency, and so this trivial game that I play continues.

Today, just like on many past visits, I get it wrong and wind up on the east side of *via Tuscolana*. Now I will have to wait for the traffic signal to change and give me permission to cross over to the other side. It is an excruciatingly long wait. To pass the time I amuse myself with the thought that soon the cars and trucks will have to wait for me. I smile as I imagine them impatiently revving their engines like packs of barking dogs as I cross in front of them. Then I see her and the barking dogs vanish.

A fire engine red *Vespa* catches my eye from the right. The very next thing I notice is her shoulder length blond hair dancing in the wind. Her four inch stiletto heels are no impediment as she deftly leans her moto into a 90 degree left through the intersection and then pops right back up as she merges into the *Tuscolana* traffic. Pretty stylish riding, I think to myself as she disappears to the south.

The traffic light finally turns green and I am liberated. As I am crossing, I can't help but feel that the Universe is smiling at me. So early in the day and already a few interesting sights and thoughts have crossed my path. I wonder what else it has in store for me today.

Arriving at the cafe, I take a *cappuccino* and a *brioche*. The place is pretty empty. The coffee was excellent today. I think briefly about indulging myself with another. I decide not to. Perhaps on my way home. I collect my small backpack and depart the café. In just over an hour from now I will meet the *Pastore Nero*. However, I do not know this yet.

After crossing *via Lemonia* and walking through the church parking lot, I veered left and picked up a trail. The park can be entered from either the left or the right of the church. I typically go left, for no particular reason, just as I did today.

I attended a funeral at that church once and it was indescribably sad. Yet in the middle of that profound sadness I was involved in an unexpected moment of incredible emotional depth. Its tender honesty caught me completely by surprise. It was a special gift that I will never forget. I am not going to share it with you because it is very personal, and in all honestly you lack the context to truly appreciate its depth.

Once inside the park, you can either head for the *Acqueducto* and walk alongside it, or take the trail to the east and enjoy the ruins from a distance. For me this choice is always influenced by the time of day, the quality of the sky, and whether or not I have a camera with me.

After I had cleared the treeline of umbrella shaped pines I saw the *Acqueducto*. The pines here are so different from those back in Canada. Here they have a certain elegance and minimalist style to them. They are like inverted pyramids and so really the opposite of the bushy green triangles that live across the pond. Also, these ones rarely see the snow. They seem happier to me than their Canadian cousins who get blanketed with the white stuff on a regular basis.

The *Acqueducto* never fails to impress me, both from far away as well as from close-up. At a distance it seems to stretch out forever as it dominates the landscape with its linear certainty. It is self-important in its pedigree, and rightly so after supplying Rome with water for millennia. No less impressive is that it is still standing, albeit in sections, over two thousand years after it was built.

Today I have decided that I will walk alongside the great walls so that I can be close to them. Other than the occasional plane overhead on its final approach to *Ciampino* airport it is very quiet in the park right now.

As I continue my trek towards the walls, I embrace this tranquility.

Then I hear the singing. It is very faint and so I have to stop and really concentrate to determine which direction it is coming from. At first I had trouble, it felt almost as confusing as how it is under water. Finally, I locked in and started moving towards it. The volume increased slightly as I drew closer, and now I perceived actual words.

I stopped for a moment to listen and was moved. The voice had a very emotive quality to it. I could have easily stood in that spot listening to her all day. Yet, I was also very curious to see the source of the voice that I was hearing. Conversely, I felt a degree of hesitation over intruding on her moment. She must be just on the other side of the *Acqueducto*. Suddenly the singing stopped, the perfect time to approach?

Once I had crossed over to the other side through one of the arches, she was about ten meters off to my left and was standing very close to the wall. It was one of the better preserved sections, two tiers high and with some of its ancient facade still intact. She looked up with intent at the wall and began singing again.

Seconds later, she paused abruptly and turned to me. Her gaze suggested that I was an intruder and so I hastily stammered out an apology. She smiled in response, her eyes became welcoming and she motioned me to approach. After exchanging the basic pleasantries, we crossed over to the other side and sat with our backs against the wall with the sun on our faces. Our view took in the valley, and in the distance *Cinecitta.*

Her name was Anna, and she was an opera singer. She told me that she liked to come here and practice singing to the walls sometimes. The walls never judged her performance she told me, with a shy smile.

In the spirit of reciprocity, that is the norm in situations such as these, I told her the basics of where I lived and what I did for work. She was very curious about Canada and asked me many questions about my life there.

Anna shared with me that one of her travel dreams was to visit Canada to see the igloos and the polar bears. When I confessed to her that I had never seen either of them she expressed a surprised disappointment.

Slight pangs of guilt began to emerge. I was taking up her practice time. I was also feeling a bit restless to continue my walk. There was more out there that I was destined to see today. We agreed to meet in a week's time at the café bar on *Pza. A.C. Sabino* and continue our conversation there. She crossed back over to her singing spot and I continued along the valley side heading south west.

There was a cloud of dust level with the horizon, off to the right and forming on the other side of the Walls. My first thought was to veer left and steer clear of it, but then I decided to walk towards it to investigate. I can't say why I made the choice that I did. Just as I did not know exactly why I decided to keep my camera out and at the ready, instead of sleeping in my backpack.

If you stop and think about it, we make these choices dozens of times a day. We choose quickly, and without much thought most of the time. Are these choices really that mundane or are we simply on autopilot? Is it instinct? Experience? A mix of both, or is it something else entirely?

Now was not the time to wrestle with those questions. I re-focused my attention. I was approaching the break in the walls; The one where the dirt road was that formed the northern boundary of the golf course. This was where the dust cloud was emanating from.

At the break I saw a large flock of sheep moving towards the aqueduct on their way to the pasture in the valley to graze. They were being managed by a medium sized black dog. A few hundred sheep yet only one dog it seemed. As the flock made its way by me, a stocky man with a switch became visible at the back of it.

Something was about to happen. I could feel that tingle of anticipation I get when the Universe wants to show me something. Suddenly, I knew why I had kept my camera available. I scrambled to get back in front of the flock. As it turned out, there was no need to hurry because they had reached the valley pastures and were grazing now.

The black dog had also stopped. It seemed to be waiting for the man to catch up. Eventually, the man did catch up and he passed the dog. The dog got up and followed the man. Both the man and the dog looked at me as I framed them up. No words were exchanged. Then they both looked away. It was in that instant that I took a photograph.

A few years later I entered that photograph in a competition. I titled it *Pastore Nero*, or Black Shepherd. That photograph received an honourable mention from the judges. I had always liked this image because its simple content was pregnant with meaning for me. In particular, a visual testament to the memories of a day in the park that was unlike any other.

After I left the flock and had traveled quite a bit farther along the walls, I saw a solitary figure in the distance. The figure was standing on a hilltop, with the valley positioned between herself and the *Acqueducto*. As I made my way closer I saw that she was not alone. She had an easel and a canvas with her.

As the distance between us decreased, I noticed that my feelings of apprehension increased. It was just as they had appeared earlier when I had approached the opera singer. Once again, here I was intruding in someone else's moment. My trepidation was unwarranted. Seeing me and then my cameras, she gave me a friendly nod as she lowered her brush and palette. I took that as a signal that I was welcome to approach.

She asked me if I was a professional photographer. I answered that I was only a serious amateur. With a smile she told me that it was the same for her with canvas and brushes.

As our conversation evolved we discovered that we were both of the same mind as to the reasons why we chose to label ourselves this way. Notwithstanding the fact that each of us earned our living outside of the arts, we also found ourselves in agreement that once money entered the equation that our relationship with our art would inevitably change, and most likely for the worst. Money can be a corrosive influence that rusts whatever it touches.

Our relationship with our respective arts was something pure and deeply personal to each of us. It was something that we believed needed to be nurtured and protected by us. This relationship was reciprocal since art provided us with a sanctuary which offered discovery and growth via creative expression.

When I had initially approached her, she had stepped out from behind her easel and then had moved in front of it. I was curious to see her painting, yet she was still positioned between me and her easel. I wondered now if this had been deliberate on her part or if it was merely an unconscious act.

As I was examining those thoughts, she asked me if I wanted to have a look at her painting. Now I wondered if she was reading my mind. Her canvas was about two thirds completed and it was stunning! I told her that she was painting the photograph that I dreamt of taking. She really seemed to appreciate that compliment. To my eyes she had really nailed it with her use of light and hues on the walls and sky.

I worked my eyes over every part of the canvas and then I saw them. Way over on the left side, near the vanishing point, there was a small flock of miniature sheep and an equally tiny *Pastore Nero*. I could not resist the temptation. I showed her the photo of *Pastore Nero* that I had recently taken and she laughed with pleasure at this coincidence.

It turned out that we were both intent on capturing the *Acqueducto*. We had approached it in different ways with different tools. Then quite by chance, we discovered that our respective creative visions were close cousins. The serendipity of our arriving at a similar destination via different paths did not escape us.

Her way was slower, and perhaps was a more deliberate way. For her it was rarely about a specific moment in time. It was more often a composite, created from a collection of moments that could span from a handful of seconds to just this side of eternity. Her way began with a blank canvas that she added her brush strokes to over time. She had the benefit of poetic license and so in a sense could reinvent history in the form of a moment that never actually existed if she chose to.

My way was also very deliberate. The process could take a long time, or it could be instantaneous. Typically, it was somewhere in between yet generally towards the longer end of the temporal spectrum. My way always began with a *'full canvas'* from which I had to judiciously subtract what did not fit the image, while simultaneously anticipating and capturing what enhanced it.

My way was pure history, the freezing of time to capture a moment that could never be exactly the same again. I had the benefit of speed and quantity on my side. I could capture many images very quickly and then later decide which one conveyed the most meaning. It was a benefit I was not convinced that I trusted, and so I only chose to use it in very specific circumstances.

The day was slowly giving way to night, and we both had other places where we needed to be sooner rather than later. She quickly packed up her gear and we walked to the *Metropolitana* together. From where we were in the park *Cinecitta* was the closest station. Our conversation lasted until she disembarked at *Colli Albani*.

We did not bother to exchange our contact information or to suggest a future get together. There was no need to do so. Instinctively we both knew that we would meet up again in the park one day soon and pick up our conversation then and there.

Now solitary, I reflected on how this visit to the park had been particularly rewarding. In fact, it was more so than any of my previous visits that I could remember. I felt invigorated and ready to return to the *Centro* now. Then I heard him. I turned to look at what I already knew that I would see: the hipster hand-talker barking into his phone with his left arm flapping about wildly.

This time he glared defiantly at me and just kept right on talking. I turned back around in my seat. I got off the train at the next station which was *Furio Camillo*. I could not have planned it any better if I had tried to. It was dinner time and Sir Enzo's *trattoria* was just down the road. My introduction to the theatre that is Sir Enzo's is a story best left for another day.

Long after I had left Rome and had returned to Canada, I had an enlarged print of *Pastore Nero* framed. It hangs on a wall in my office. It feels right to me to have an image of those ancient walls hanging up on my modern wall. It is my path back to that eternal day.

The Poetry of a Small Bird

I stepped onto the balcony and surveyed the life below on *via Nardones** in the *Quartieri*. Sometimes, my visits here were purely as a voyeur. More often though, the balcony was where I came to lose myself in thought. On those times, the life unfolding below me was merely white noise; a welcome distraction for my eyes.

My television had stopped working years ago, and it was too ancient to repair. I decided that I could not afford to replace it. It was a question of time, and not of money. Time spent in front the television is time not spent living in the world. The balcony had become my surrogate television, and I found it to be far more interesting than actual television had ever been.

The brightness of a sudden realization lit up my face. I could not see that, though I most certainly felt it. My mind was curious about a recent event, yet completely untroubled by it. A chance meeting that did not actually occur; a near-miss that managed to leave an interesting ripple effect in its wake.

The importance of time in the equation was striking to me. Had we arrived a minute earlier, the chance meeting would have certainly transpired. Arriving one minute later, the chance to meet would not have even existed. By all appearances, it seemed as if the meeting was not supposed to occur, but rather was simply a visual portal into her

* See Glossary P.192

15

troubled past.

In the aftermath, once her initial shock had subsided, she shared with me what had almost happened as well as her relief that it had not actually happened. As we had pulled into the parking lot of the restaurant she had seen a ghost from her past. She did not share any more than that; and instead grew distant as she retreated into the silence of her memories.

A few days later, I returned to that meeting that never was. Although my frame of reference was contextually lacking, I was able to reach a speculative conclusion. It was the best outcome that I could have hoped for under the circumstances. What I decided was that the ghost that I had almost met had made the most serious mistake.

Of course I had also made this grievous error in my distant past. Most men have. Some men never learn from this mistake, while others never recover from it. That man-ghost had taken for granted the love of a woman. I am of the opinion that this is the greatest sin that a man can make.

Tangentially, I wished that I could meet the man. Not in that past moment of the meeting that almost was. Now, after I had had some time alone with my thoughts, would be a good moment. Truly, it was of no major importance. It was merely that I was curious and had questions that I would like to ask him. I also felt a strong wish to thank this man for his sin. For without it, she may have never stepped into my life.

The delicious irony that we had recently discovered together was that we had previously stepped into each other lives in a peripheral way. There had been an event where we had been in the same room for several hours. There were other people there. That was many years ago and we had not been ready for each other in that moment.

It was a distinct possibility that over the ensuing years we had been in several other places at the same time. Perhaps we had even exchanged a smile or a brief glance; or more likely nothing at all. It was impossible to say for certain. The faded memories of decades past are often frustratingly inaccessible.

The moment when the blue light of the early evening gradually blackens into night is my favourite time of day. This transition signaled to me that her arrival was imminent. The night often brought her to me; the morning then took her away. With a few notable exceptions it had been this way since we had joined together. One day this would change and she would be with me always and forever. That dream was a very pleasant one for me.

Very soon after I had met her, there were moments throughout the day when the memories of her arrived. These memories pushed the other thoughts out of my mind, and radiated contentment into my heart. Sometimes, it was the memories of when we were in the rapture of discovering each other; when it felt brand new and so very special to both of us. Other times, it was the memory of her sparkling green eyes in the moonlight; or of how the softness of the candlelight lit up her face in love. Revisiting these memories, I felt the warmth of her moving through my core. She was a wonderful gift that left me feeling blessed, humbled and amazed at what her presence had brought into my life.

The profound meaning of this gift was explicitly clear to me. I recalled the period, without rancor, of what I had nick-named *The Great Unpleasantness*. That term was part of a line from a movie that I was fond of and had enjoyed many times. This period in my life was initially full of promise and hope; a new beginning. Then the promises were broken, and the hope vanished. It turned out that the promises had always been only empty words. What followed was a period of soul-searching and healing. It was towards the end of that period that the gift of her was bestowed upon me. I was ready.

A small bird passed by, distracting me from my thoughts of her. It came to rest at a feeder on a neighbouring balcony. This bird was very small; perhaps only a third the size of the other birds that normally visited that feeder. What would happen if one of those other birds came along now? I knew exactly what would happen, and I felt sad. I did not enjoy being reminded of the cruel injustices that populate daily life. The small bird was perfection. It was a tiny delicate beauty that the larger birds could never hope to equal.

Losing interest in the fate of the small bird my thoughts returned to the man. Perhaps that man was blind in a metaphorical sense, and so he did not see what he had lost. More likely though, he never realized what he had actually had.

Love can be just like that small bird I mused. True love is tiny and delicate in its beauty; it is quiet poetry. Love is also fragile and consequently fleeting; and very easy to miss if you do not know how to see it.

Did that man know how to see it? I would never be able to answer that question. Only the man could answer that question; provided of course that he even recognized its existence. It is an absolute truth that many questions have no answers. This question was not one of them.

With the approaching blackness of night came the cold. The stiff chill of a late summer breeze signaled an approaching transition. It was not quite the time for the leaves to change their colours; it would be soon though. There would not be many more nights on the balcony of this duration available to me, I concluded. The small bird had left the feeder. I was alone.

Pushing those inconsequential thoughts away, I returned to her. She had not arrived yet; however, she was not late. I remembered the day I decided to let go of fear. It was suffocating me and putting all that I hoped for at risk. If I was a prisoner, was she my freedom?

On that day, I decided that love was the better choice than fear.

Intellectually, it was the only choice. Emotionally, it was much less clear for me. Even though I had made my decision, it turned out that the struggle of the heart and mind was not over for either of us as yet.

Neither she nor I were aware of this struggle in that precise moment. We awoke to its existence shortly thereafter. Theories are not always truths, even though it sometimes feels like they are. I knew this, yet I often forgot it.

She had still not arrived, and now she was a little bit late. I was not worried. I had my thoughts to keep me company until she reached the apartment. I went inside to grab a jacket, and to make a coffee. Those two items would buy me some more time on the balcony as the night blackened and the temperature made its gradual descent.

As I was waiting on the coffee, I looked around my apartment. It was small, yet it was enough space for me at this juncture of my life. I reminisced about some of the places that I had inhabited over the years. Invariably, I came back to my current abode which was situated in the *Quartieri Spagnoli* neighbourhood of Naples.

I had to remind myself that in ascending to a higher level of feeling, it was only natural that I no longer wanted to go back to where I had started. It would be too simple and unfulfilling back there, now that I had tasted a deeper and more complex reality with her.

From among all of the places in which I had lived, I decided that I liked this small apartment the best. It was my home, in a way that was distinctly different from all of the others that had come before it. This was not so much due to the actual apartment itself, but moreover the result of its location in the vibrant *Quartieri*.

Love had brought me to a path of beauty and discovery. At this level the air is thinner, the landscape changes quickly, and I could easily loose the path. That thought was a disconcerting paradox – the fear of loss in the midst of such beauty.

The *moka's* burbling shriek signaled that the coffee was ready. I carefully picked it up and poured the *doppio* espresso into a conventional sized coffee mug. This action did not seem the least bit strange to me. My friend of many years Luca would not have agreed. I snatched up my jacket from where it had been resting on the left arm of the couch, and returned to the balcony.

Even though she had still not arrived at the apartment yet, she was with me out there on the balcony. She was always with me now, even when she was not physically present. I had made space for her in both my heart and in my mind. The imprint of her love on me was very deep.

She was late now. Instinctively, I turned and raised my arm to check the time. Even before this action was completed I knew that it was futile. I could not recall the exact period when I had forsaken wearing a watch. Time moved on whether or not I chose to keep track of it. I had chosen not to, and as it turned out my life had become simpler as a result of this choice.

As I sipped my coffee on the balcony, I recalled that I had dreamt of two women last night. However, they did not appear at the same time. There were two different dreams on the same night. One of the women was her. She represented the Now. I remembered thinking how ironic it was to be dreaming about the woman who was lying next to me in that very moment. I was not sure if that thought was part of the dream, or if it was an actual conscious thought in a state of semi-wakefulness.

After the dream, when I awoke and saw her there, I marveled at her beauty. The quietness of the new day was among the moments when she was the most striking to me. In that briefest of moments we belonged only to each other, in an affirmation of the poetry that lived between us. This was before the day separated us with its myriad of demands and obligations.

The other dream was about a woman from my past. I had not dreamt about her in over a decade. That dream was so vivid that it left me slightly troubled. I could not help but wonder what triggered my subconscious to go so deep into the archives and deliver this ghost to me after such a lengthy absence. Afterwards, it felt strange to me to have seen her again in this way. Only a few days removed from it, I did not recall any significant details of that dream. I was now unsure if it was even her ghost.

The true meaning of these concurrent dreams escaped me. What was the message that they were sending? There were so many potential meanings; I would never be able to narrow it down to just one. It will remain forever as an unfinished story for me; a mystery that will never be solved.

I heard a faint knock at the front door, and so came in from the balcony to answer it. At first I thought it was her. As I strode across the apartment to the door I wondered why she would knock when she had a key. Upon reaching the foyer, I flicked the light on, opened the deadbolt, and then turned the doorknob to open the door. There was no one there. I leaned over the threshold and peered down the hallway. It was empty. She was very late now.

Was I hearing things again? The heavy click of the stairwell door confirmed that I was not. Someone had knocked on my door and then exited via the stairwell. I was uncertain about what to do next. I decided to go back out on my balcony and watch the main entrance three floors below. Less than a minute later a man exited the apartment building.

I got a good look at the man, but I did not recognize him. The man appeared to be close in age to me. He was well-dressed and moved quickly; yet with a fluid purpose as opposed to erratic haste. The man crossed the street and entered the café on the corner. I briefly thought about going to confront him there. I decided against doing so; instead choosing to remain in the sanctuary of my balcony. As it turned out, the man soon exited the café and vanished around the corner. I would not have had enough time to reach him.

The parallel was not lost on me. This was another meeting that never happened. I wondered about these similar yet unrelated events. What if they actually were related in some unseen way? I could not help following the path of speculation to its inevitable conclusion; that the man was the same one on both of the occasions that I had almost met him. The odds of such an occurrence were infinitesimal. Still, truth is often stranger than fiction...isn't it?

What did the man want? Why did he knock and then immediately leave? In the final analysis, it did not matter. What did matter was that she had still not arrived. I was not used to this feeling of worry. Her punctuality was normally such that I could set my watch by it. Except that I no longer wore a watch. Television would have been useful now I thought. I could have watched the news to learn if there were accidents or delays with the subway system. Without this I could only continue my solitary vigil for her.

For several years now I had no longer had any interest in time. Perhaps this was why I so often lost track of it. The darkness was growing marginally lighter. I had been awake all night. It is more likely that I had dozed periodically, as was my habit, in the comfort of the long chair with the ample cushions. I simply liked to think that I had been awake the entire night. A strange little lie I told myself; even though I was aware of the truth. Such harmless little delusions often served to keep me amused.

As the dawn grew incrementally stronger I saw the small bird return to the feeder. The perfect beauty of the small creature filled me with awe and gratitude. Nature's poetry was alive and on display in the small bird, was the thought that reached me in that moment. In the quiet of the morning, before the others awoke, this moment belonged only to the small bird and I. This was very similar to how it was with her. Having these instances of poetry in my life was very important; for through them I was nourished.

Then I heard the key strike the lock, the deadbolt turn over and the creak of the door as it opened. I quickly rose from the long chair and went to greet her. My heart felt warm and peaceful. I was ready to receive her; and was excited to join her in our embrace.

As the door to my apartment began to open. the alarm rang and jolted me awake. A brutal signal that it was time to begin another day. I silenced the alarm and then rolled over to find her there beside me.

The day would soon snatch her from me, as it always did. In those quiet moments of a new day, before it would take her, I gazed upon her sleeping in the poetry of her beauty. How was I to know that this would be the last time that I would enjoy her in this way?

Trattoria no. 2

It is a pretty nondescript little place as far as appearances go. If it wasn't for the large vertical neon sign hanging above it you could easily walk right past it. In fact, I have noticed that most people do walk right past it. I think that it is because people rarely look up while they are walking. People are always in a hurry nowadays, even in Rome.

There are only four tables perched out on the sidewalk in front of the little place, and they are always occupied. That could be another reason why people always seem to walk past the little place.

I myself have passed this place many times on my way to and from *Termini** station. I have even photographed its retro neon sign a few times at night. It has a simple white glow that calls out from the darkness, like a beacon leading to an oasis. In a classic black and white image it is absolute perfection; evoking a Rome of a bygone era. Fellini's *la Dolce Vita* era to be exact.

In today's Rome, this original has somehow managed to survive in spite of its being virtually engulfed by Chinese shoe stores that never seem to have any customers, kebab joints, and shops full of tacky plastic crap. That is what they call progress, or alternately shrug off as natural evolution. This so-called *'progress'* seems more akin to entropy in my view.

See Glossary P.192

Change is not always for the better. That is just my opinion; about some things...not all things, but definitely some things. Oftentimes, it is not until we lose something that we are able to gain a true appreciation of it, and of what it meant to us. Too late, as by then it is gone. Nothing is going to bring it back and we are now forced to be satisfied with our fading memories of it as we think it once was.

Ironically, when enough time has passed it may sort of come back. Not the simple authentic and pure expression of it that vanished long ago, but rather a modern imitation of it playing the nostalgia angle. It is like a time machine that may rekindle old memories and generate new ones; for a price of course. However, it is only in the rarest of instances that this second edition can even approximate the original, let alone equal it.

As I approached the little place, on my way home from *Termini* of course, I see a miracle...a free table...today is my day! I take a seat and moments later I am given a menu. I order an *antipasto*, a *primi*, and a glass of *Nero d'Avola*.

To this day I can't order a glass without remembering that I have still not made it down to Sicily yet. Next year I say to myself, as I have on many previous occasions. *Liar! My self answers me back with conviction.* Curious how these little broken promises travel with us through the years isn't it? Very few of us ever hold ourselves accountable for the promises that we whisper to ourselves. Some of them become broken promises; while the majority of them are simply forgotten.

The waiter brings the wine. He seems a little too gracious in his demeanor and leaves me wondering why he is trying so hard. The wine is good and it lingers nicely on the palate. I smile at my internal dialogue which is already making the case for a second glass of this exquisite nectar. When in Rome!

My reverie was suddenly interrupted by a shadow falling across my table, which was followed by a rather insistent throat-clearing noise. I looked up to identify the source of the shadow as being a little Old Man with a silvery grey mustache. He sported a dated navy blue suit, slightly rumpled but overall it seemed only gently used. What was he after?

Now that he had claimed my attention he spoke to me. It was in a dialect that I could not grasp. I shrugged my shoulders and turned my palms upwards to gesture that I did not understand what he was saying. The Old Man became slightly flustered, and then a little agitated. He repeated his words, only this time a bit slower and with an added degree of care it seemed. Once he had finished speaking his expression became hopeful that the communication gap had now been bridged. It had not been.

Fortuitously, the waiter appeared to rescue us from our awkward linguistic stalemate. He apologetically informed me that it was his mistake. As it turned out, I was in the Old Man's seat and he was asking me to move. With that clarification I turned my gaze back to the Old Man. Where his expression had been hopeful only moments ago, I now saw a distinct pleading look in his eyes. How could I refuse this request?

I stood up and asked the waiter where I was moving to. Before he could answer me, the Old Man motioned the waiter in close so that he could whisper something to him. The waiter smiled as he straightened up and told me:

"You do not have to change tables, only your seat. The gentleman has invited you to join him for lunch." then he added: *"He has been having lunch here every Thursday for the past thirty years; always at this table and always in this seat. Today it slipped my mind. I should never have seated you here. It's entirely my fault; how about another glass on the house?"*

I accepted the offer because I respect tradition, and personal rituals. Also, the Old Man struck me as an interesting character and so the thought crossed my mind that to join him might just prove to be better than dining alone, again. Perhaps this would turn out to be true for both of us.

I asked the waiter to inform the Old Man that I understood and that it would be my pleasure to join him. The waiter explained, and I gave the Old Man a big smile. In response a look of immense relief radiated from his eyes. They were piercingly blue, and they now seemed to sparkle with an even greater intensity in the midday light.

It has been my experience that often it takes very little to make people very happy. Sometimes, it takes even less to make them very angry. There is no denying the fact that people are irrational animals that all too frequently find themselves at the mercy of their emotions.

The waiter brought the menu and the Old Man said *"Merci Monsieur!"* with a stylish flourish.

"Ah, vous parlez Francais Monsieur?" I asked him.

"Mais bien sur Monsieur!" he replied.

With that simple exchange we had found some common ground, and so now a whole range of conversational possibilities had opened up for us. The natural starting point was to satisfy our mutual curiosity as to how the other had found their way to the French language. For me the answer was simple: a French Canadian mother more or less made the language my birthright. On that foundation was added years of study in school to produce the desired result of fluency.

The Old Man congratulated me on my good fortune, and then he revealed that his path to the French language was born out of necessity. A post-war gamble based on reasons he was not prepared to divulge at that moment, he explained. Perhaps at some point in the future, he added. Fair enough I thought.

I asked the Old Man if it was true that he had had lunch at this very table every Thursday for the past thirty years. With a knowing smile he told me that he had, and then he deftly shifted the focus off himself by asking what had brought me to Rome.

Nothing in particular I replied. I went on to share with him that I have been getting to know the Eternal City for years; although not for as long as he had been having lunch at this table. The Old Man emitted a wise chuckle and told me that even a lifetime is not enough to truly know Rome.

I asked the Old Man what he had seen in his lifetime in Rome. The Old Man immediately corrected me that he had not spent a lifetime in Rome but only the last thirty years.

"*Well certainly the last thirty years were pretty interesting in Rome?*" I inquired.

"*Perhaps they were.*" replied the Old Man.

This was getting to be like pulling teeth I thought to myself. I said nothing and the Old Man saw that I was waiting for him to continue.

"*Do you know Italian cinema?*" he asked me.

"*A little bit*" I replied.

"*So you know Fellini?*"

"Sure, I know Fellini. Well truly, I do not know Fellini as I have never met the man, but I do know of him."

"I used to cut his hair."

"What... you're kidding me!"

"Back in the early 1960's one of my jobs was at a barber shop on Via Veneto." he said.

At that point the Old Man paused, and looked off into the distance as he decided how much he was going to share with me.

"There is not much to say. It was only a few times. He did not talk much at all; mostly just read la Republica while I was cutting. In any case that was not my favorite job that I had in Rome."

"Which was your favorite?" I asked him.

"Well, it was my first one of course. It was special because I had just begun making a new life for myself in Rome. Do you want to know why I come to this restaurant every Thursday?"

Then the Old Man leaned in towards me, quickly glanced around to see if the waiter was near, and lowered his voice as he explained:

"Honestly, it is not for the food that I come back. No, it is because this is where it all started for me in Rome. I had no money. The owner gave me meals on credit while I looked for work. After a couple of weeks, when I could not find any work the owner gave me my first job. Washing dishes and cleaning the place in exchange for food and a place to sleep. This little trattoria is my roots in Rome. It just feels necessary to come back here every week. It began as a pilgrimage of sorts, and now after so many years it is a comfortable and necessary habit."

The Old Man paused, leaned back into his chair and took a brief look down the street.

"I did not wash the dishes for long. Very soon I was doing his job."

The Old Man nodded in the direction of the waiter who was approaching our table with the antipasti.

"That was how I met my wife."

He said as he picked up his fork and speared a marinated artichoke heart from his plate. I followed his lead and tucked into my antipasto.

We were quiet for a while. The waiter brought some bread. There is nothing like Roman bread. The good stuff has a tough outer crust that tears up the roof of your mouth a few times until you get used to it. This bread was perfect for doing *la scarpetta,* or literally the little shoe.

No one has ever been able to explain this expression to me, though I have asked several people. As a result what the linkage is between mopping up pasta sauce from your plate with a crust of bread and little shoes is still a riddle to me.

Doing *la scarpetta*, especially with Elide's homemade sauce, is one of the things I look forward to the most on every visit I make to Rome. What began as a pilgrimage for me is now a comfortable habit after so many visits. I am similar to the Old Man in this respect.

The Old Man looked up from his now empty plate with a satisfied smile as he reached for his glass of wine. He took a sip and asked me if I knew of the writer Italo Calvino. I replied in the affirmative and told him that my introduction to Calvino was the result of a gift from a wise professor from *Napoli*.

It was the first gift that she gave me: Calvino's *The Nonexistent Knight and The Cloven Viscount*. The book was accompanied by a rather cryptic personal note advising me that I would see elements of myself in the book if I looked carefully enough. She did not specify if it was the Knight or the Viscount that reminded her of me. I read those two stories but I did not see any resemblance. I kept forgetting to ask her to elaborate on her note. We have not been in touch for years, and so it remains a sweet mystery.

"I also enjoyed those stories very much. Especially The Cloven Viscount." The Old Man stated. He went on: *"I dabbled with writing for many years.*

Short stories mostly, but I never got very far with them. Many great ideas but after three or four paragraphs I would always get stalled."

"Writing well is not easy. It is a gift." I offered. "I also enjoyed those stories but my favorite by Calvino is The Baron in the Trees."

"Yes, the Baron was a very good story, charmingly absurd in my opinion. The one of his that I liked the best was The Path to the Spiders' Nests because it reminds me of my time in the Resistance during the war. That story of Calvino's causes memories to surface that inevitably take me back to France after the war. I was very happy there, for a while at least, but that is a story for another day."

He paused there, and looked out towards the street. I remained silent. Intuitively sensing that he needed some time to return from where the poignant emotion of that memory had just taken him.

"Where were we?" the Old Man asked me after he had come back.

"Writing well." I replied.

"Ah yes. Well in any case I can tell you with certainty that very few things are easy in life. Once you get to my age you will know this to be true."

The Old Man's words carried a measured degree of gravitas. After speaking them he looked away again. This time it was to let his words linger with me for a moment. Suddenly, he leaned over and grabbed my arm to get my attention and direct it across the street.

"See that man over there? The one in the ratty grey suit, standing in front of the shoe store?" the Old Man asked. Before I could reply he quickly went on. *"He was one of my unfinished stories. Staples Man."*

"Staples Man?" I inquired quizzically.

"Yes, Staples Man. We were colleagues working in the same municipal office years ago. It was very uninteresting clerical work, paper shuffling to be honest. Anyhow my colleague, that man across the street, had worked in that department for many years. It turns out that he had a most unusual secret."

The Old Man had leaned in and whispered this to me. Given the fact that Staples man was across the street the Old Man's level of discretion seemed completely unnecessary to me.

"One day, he decided to share his secret with me. In one of the drawers of his desk there was a black plastic basket of medium size."

And the Old Man gestured with his hands to show me the approximate size of the black basket.

"In the basket was a heaping pile of staples. Every staple from every document that had ever passed across his desk my colleague informed me. Twenty-seven years worth of staples as it turned out. Incredible!"

He paused to take a sip of wine. I did the same.

The Old Man returned to his story and told me that a few weeks later he noticed that this colleague had used staples to hem up his pants. Naturally he asked his colleague:

"Shouldn't those staples be in the basket?"

The colleague replied:

"No, these are internal staples, from the municipal department, so it is appropriate for me to use them to hem my pants. It would be most inappropriate, because they are internal staples, to put then into the basket. In fact, it would be absolutely ludicrous to do so. There are rules you know. Only external staples from citizens' documents can be added into the basket."

The Old Man chuckled softly at this memory before he went on to tell me more about his colleague.

"I remember that his eyes were riveted to me after he had spoken. He needed to study my reaction to determine if I had clearly understood this critical distinction: not all staples were of equal importance. I remember nodding in agreement and smiling at him. My colleague seemed satisfied that I had understood. Then he picked up his staple puller and turned his attention back to the pile of papers on his desk."

The Old Man paused briefly here, perhaps deciding in which direction to take the story next.

"That incident got me wondering. In fact, now that I think about it, all these years later it still makes me wonder." The Old Man said. *"He never told me why he was collecting the staples. Of course, I felt it was impolite to ask him for an explanation. So I never did."* Then the Old Man asked me point blank: *"Do you think this was madness?"*

"Well, I certainly do not see any evidence of genius. However, I do not think that it qualifies as madness either. In this particular instance I will go with mildly eccentric with a side order of obsessive-compulsive." I replied. *"Is there more to the story? What happened with the basket of staples?"*

"Honestly, I do not have an answer for you. A year or so later I was transferred to a different division in an office located in another part of the city. I never saw Staples man again; until today that is."

"Perhaps we should venture across the street and ask him about his basket of staples?"

I said this with an exaggerated smile. The Old Man caught on immediately.

"No. I do not think that we will be doing that today. Besides, here comes our primi."

He replied as he adjusted his napkin on his lap and picked up his fork as the waiter delivered our plates from his tray to our table.

A comfortable silence descended upon us once again. The aroma of the food was intoxicating! Pausing between bites I looked back across the street and noticed that Staples man was gone. Turning my attention back to my plate I briefly wondered if the Old man might now decide to finish writing that story.

A bit later, as he removed our empty plates, the waiter inquired if we desired an aperitif or a coffee. The Old Man took the liberty of ordering us a couple of *limoncellos* and espressos.

"We are in for a treat. The limoncello is homemade. From the owner's recipe using the best lemons from his cousin's farm in Campania." the Old Man explained.

The Old Man pushed his chair back a bit from the table and turned it slightly so that he could stretch his legs out, and get a better view of the street life. He had the right idea I concluded.

As I followed suit my napkin fell to the ground. Reaching down to pick it up, a very bright but very small glint caught my eye. I had to lean in a little closer to identify its source. It was from the sun hitting the staples that were hemming the Old Man's pants.

The Gifts

A *Metropolitana** ride in Rome only rarely provides any occurrences worthy of mention. However, today was the exception. It happened while I was making my way to the *Centro* to meet a friend for lunch. Yes, today most certainly was an extraordinary exception.

Two or three stops from the *Guila Agricola* station, where I had embarked, a scruffy teen carrying a really beat-up acoustic guitar joined our car. Four strings where there should have been six, a small chunk missing from the bottom edge, neck dented and missing frets.

My eyes moved from the guitar to the kid. Ratty old sneakers with two different colour laces, a stained t-shirt several sizes too large hanging limply and covered by a tattered denim jacket. The entire ensemble was crowned by a straw fedora that had seen better days. It was hard to decide which one was in rougher shape, the kid or the guitar. In time such judgments became meaningless, as they typically do.

The kid immediately took ownership of our *Metropolitana* car. This was not your standard greasy haired, grey-toothed, stubbled and off-key accordion player paired with a grimy faced child to guilt us into parting with our coins. No, this was something different. The kid began playing a familiar tune whose name escapes me now. It was how he played that forgotten song that hypnotized those of us in the

See Glossary P.193

subway car that day.

He went so deep into his performance, forgetting about us, where he was, and in a sense himself. Completely absorbed by the moment, he could have been anywhere, playing for anyone or for no one. The few times he looked up his face was a mask of focused passion, seemingly oblivious to the audience that he had captivated.

The kid definitely worked the car but that was unintentional. Dancing about with his instrument, they each took turns leading. It was an expression of his pure *bodhisattva* nature to give us that moment.

The spell was broken upon our arrival at *Termini* station. The kid stopped playing and resurfaced. Our moment with him was now fixed in time. The doors opened, we stepped onto the platform and became scattered diaspora. Each of us now fixated solely on the next move in our respective journeys.

My journey took me past *Piazza Republica* to *via Alessandria* and the *Cafe Monte Carlo* that was near Luca's office. The cafe was empty save for two *baristas* who were deeply engrossed in the pale pink pages of a *Gazetta de la Sport*. I approached the bar and politely requested: "*Un cafe per favore.*"

With exaggerated effort one of them pried himself away from the newspaper and sullenly moved towards the *macchina*. Still pouting he muttered to his *amico* that it was just his rotten luck to be serving another damn *Americano*! The other *barista* snorted in agreement and thumbed a pink page over.

Time for a little fun! I slammed my palm down onto the bar and loudly proclaimed *"No sono Americano. Sono Canadese!"* The one making my coffee flushed slightly with embarrassment and began to mumble an apology. My quick burst of laughter in reply was meant to show that all was forgiven. He delivered my coffee with a forced smile that betrayed a trace of annoyance at my recent attempt at humour.

As if on cue, Luca arrived and greeted me warmly. The *baristas* noticeably perked up in response to this event. Perhaps, I reasoned, they have elevated me on the social ladder? No such luck I realize while watching Luca exchange greetings with them. This cafe is a client of his bank, and he is their loans officer. Evidently, it has dawned on the *baristas* that if I tell Luca about their earlier *faux-pas*, then they could be in hotter water than they use to make the espressos!

It became a challenge for me to keep a straight face as I watched the *baristas* fawn over Luca. They told him how lucky he is to have a *molto simpatico amico Canadese* whom they have only just met yet already feel closer to than their own cousins.

"Are you sure he's really Canadese and not Italiano?" They ask. *"Not even a little bit? Well he could be, couldn't he? Of course he could!"*

Suspicions aroused by their animated chatter Luca downs his espresso, takes my arm and steers me out to the sidewalk as he throws the *baristas* a *"Grazie. A Presto!"*

I can only manage a couple of strides from the cafe before I am convulsed with laughter. *"Give"* says Luca. Getting myself back under control I tell him of the little drama that played out prior to his appearance. Relishing the twist that his arrival contributed, I was certain that he was already plotting the torment of the *baristas* on a future visit. I admonished him to lay off them or I wouldn't be able to take coffee there ever again.

"Roberto, why do you seek to deny me my entertainments?" he asked with exaggerated seriousness.

I press him to find other avenues for his amusement. He grudgingly agrees, and yet I'm not entirely convinced that I can trust him to keep his word. No matter, there are plenty of other cafes in Roma I remind myself.

As we navigate the *sanpietrini* towards *Termini* Luca abandons the café drama and shifts gears to the topic of our pending lunch.

"I have a real treat in store for you today my friend." he exclaimed. *"Have you ever been to Sir Enzo's?"* he inquired in an overly innocent tone.

"*Doesn't ring a bell, but we've been to lots of places over the decades, so it is possible.*" I replied.

"*Hmmm! No, I think if you'd ever been to see Sir Enzo you would not forget the experience. So it's settled then. You've never been so we're going there now.*" He exclaimed while glancing at his watch.

"*What's so special about this place?*" I inquired suspiciously.

"*Aspeta! You'll find out soon enough.*" Luca replied with a sly smile that I recognized immediately as his tell. He was plotting something.

No little Elvis on the subway this time; just a train carrying a sparse collection of noon hour commuters. Six stops later we arrive at *Furio Camillo* station and emerge from it onto a small piazza framed by non-descript apartment buildings.

"*There's nothing here. You've tricked me!*" I muttered with mock indignation.

"*See that small yellow sign with black letters off to the left about a block and a half up?*" Luca pointed to direct my attention, "*That's Sir Enzo's.*"

It was not a far walk, nor was it an interesting walk. The urban sprawl of the 1960's dominated the landscape. That extremely uninspired, yet economic, architecture that was needed to efficiently meet the housing needs of a rapidly growing city.

On the basis of the visual evidence presented, I am becoming increasing skeptical about Luca's selection today. However, in all the years I have known Luca I have observed a trait in him as immutable as the law of gravity; he is a man who is serious about food! As such, logic would dictate that he would not make the considerable effort to venture all the way out to the suburbs for a lunch of dubious quality.

"Here we are!" Luca exclaimed triumphantly as he opened the door and beckoned me to enter.

I have seen this many, many times before. Luca is up to something. He seems more amplified than usual, agitated even. Time will reveal all, just as it always has in the past. Stay in the game and keep your eyes and ears open, I reminded myself.

Sir Enzo's restaurant is most accurately described as part museum and part restaurant. It is a veritable time capsule that transports you back to the Rome of the early 1960's. Wood and more wood is the prevailing theme. Chairs, tables, bar, shelving and wainscoting all in that ubiquitous and dated shade of brown that masks the grain. There are several vintage *Peroni* posters that add a tinge of colour, but even they are not enough to overcome the stale heaviness of the brown that pervades the joint. Honestly, I can tell you that I would not have given this place a second look if I had chanced to walk past it on my own.

Clearly struggling to suppress his glee Luca awaits what he expects will be my predictable reaction. I take the contrarian route and disappoint my friend with as big a smile as I can manage and proclaim: *"Looks great. Let's eat!"* I have to get my shots in where I see an opening.

A grand total of three customers are in the *trattoria* as we enter and swell the clientele to a lunch rush of five. This solitary table consists of an older woman, a young woman and a young man.

At another table, at the rear of the room, sits a rotund man with a balding monk's fringe of *sale e pepe* hair. He is wearing cook's whites and a very sour expression. *Pince-nez* glasses clamped down at the end of his nose, as he studiously reviews the football stats in his newspaper.

"Sir Enzo." Luca whispers to me.

As we settle in at a table Sir Enzo barks out a command. In response the three customers magically transform into staff. This event reveals that Luca and I are the only patrons in the place.

A thought intrudes: Isn't there some unwritten rule about eating in restaurants where there are no other clients? Push that thought away. Keep the faith. A tattered and faded photocopy of a handwritten menu is delivered to us by the older woman.

"Order the bucatini all' amatriciana" Luca advises me. I have only just

begun to glance at the menu. His suggestion was provided in a tone that was flimsy camouflage for what was actually a command.

Apparently my friend is taking me on a journey; guiding me along a path to an experience he wants me to live. Luca is generously gifting me with a memory that we will reminisce about years from now. Another series of brush-strokes added to the rich canvas of our friendship.

Soft weeping intrudes on my thoughts. The young woman is seated again, now at a table immediately adjacent to the bar and thus hidden from Sir Enzo's view. She is sobbing quietly. I wonder if she is his daughter. She is joined by the young man who attempts to console her.

The older woman reappears at our table to take our order. With a slight nod she glides away without making a sound to deliver the order to Sir Enzo. Grunting with the effort, and a hint of annoyance, Sir Enzo rises up from his newspaper and shuffles slowly towards the kitchen area.

Judiciously seizing the opportunity presented by Sir Enzo now being in the kitchen, the young man attempts to coax the young woman to exit the restaurant. Successful in the art of persuasion, he quickly leads her to the front door. During that process he throws several nervous glances back towards the kitchen door. They make it out to the sidewalk and with a turn to the left they disappear from view.

Suddenly the proverbial light bulb flickers to life, illuminating what has until this precise moment been residing in the shadows:

"We are at the Teatro!" I whisper to Luca.

"Esattamente, you got it!" he replies with a satisfied smile.

With Sir Enzo still in the kitchen, Luca shares with me a few highlights from his previous visits here. His tales are interrupted by Sir Enzo emerging from the kitchen with a block of *pancetta* gripped in his meaty hand as he proceeds to the slicer on the bar.

"Watch this!" Luca uttered in a barely audible murmur.

Placing the *pancetta* in the slicer, and then wiping his hand on his apron, Sir Enzo adjusts his *pince-nez* and flicks the ignition switch to bring the slicer to life. After a calculated pause to ensure that we are watching him, Sir Enzo cuts the first slice. With exaggerated drama he holds the slice of *pancetta* aloft for inspection. He tilts it to and fro, as if he were a scholar examining a *Caravaggio*. Satisfied, he places the slice on a small plate and then cuts a single additional slice. With two slices now on the small plate he turns off the slicer and grabs the block of *pancetta*. Then with a stylish flourish he scoops up the plate containing the slices and strides officiously back into the kitchen.

"No one but Sir Enzo is allowed in the kitchen. That is the rule, and that is

why it takes longer than forever to get your meal!" Luca advised me and quickly added: *"Of course sometimes you get to enjoy some Teatro while you are waiting!"*

As we are now in the intermission between acts our conversation turns to other topics. Good conversation is the barometer of a friendship. Over the years we have never been at a loss for words, Luca and I.

Eventually our meal arrives, and so now the spotlight shines upon us. We have been transformed from audience members to actors in this *Teatro*. The play's main protagonist, Sir Enzo, has returned to his table and seemingly to his football stats.

In actuality, he is covertly watching the relationship evolve between us and his food. As we are both famished, we embrace our roles and dig into the meal with gusto. No acting is necessary as the food is delicious and so our reactions are genuine. Sir Enzo seems pleased with the results of his culinary efforts and returns his full attention to his newspaper.

At a table, on the opposite side of the restaurant, the older woman sits alone. She stares vacantly out the window to the uncrowded piazza. Her eyes are deep pools of despair.

A Room with no Door

I have just bridged the gap between sleep and wakefulness. As I look back I see *Morpheus** waving to me as he says: *"See you soon!"*

Pushing myself upright, to a seated position, I begin to take stock of my surroundings. They are unfamiliar to me, and thus somewhat unsettling. Nervously I scan the room from top to bottom and from side to side. I get no definitive answers from these efforts. Perhaps there will be some if I try again. I take a more determined and studied second look in a 360 degree panorama.

I am searching for a reference point that will enable me to establish my here and now. It quickly becomes apparent that there are no anchors to tether me to the comfort of familiarity that I seek. I have never been in this room before. Waking up in a strange place that I do not recognize feels like the beginning of a nightmare. I briefly wonder why my reaction in this particular instance seems so extreme, and therefore excessive.

This is a great room, of that there is no doubt. Honestly, it is beyond magnificent! It must be a *palazzo* of some sort, or maybe a museum? The floors are a stunning display of colourful marble tile mosaics of intricate geometric perfection. Above them hangs three massive crystal chandeliers spaced at equidistant intervals. Each of them is surrounded by ornate frescoes and elaborate millwork that rival that

*See Glossary P.195

found on the walls.

Also, there is a tasteful mix of paintings and sculptures placed to advantage throughout the room. Gilded millwork frames crimson coloured wall panels that each provides a home to a painting. Priceless Masterpieces? Who can say? None of them are readily identifiable to me. That is certainly not meant to imply that I claim any expertise in this area.

However, in spite of its elegant splendor, I can't help feeling that there is something not quite right about this room. That feeling inevitably leads me to question why am I so uncomfortable in such opulent surroundings? Some questions are destined to remain unanswered.

Two official looking types stride into the room. They each wear the basic dark grey suit indicative of a mid-level manager of a *Ministerio*. No one of any consequence...messengers basically. The only mark of individuality that they have been allowed is their colourful silk ties, a blue one and a red one, respectively.

They walk quickly towards me and stop less than a metre from where I am standing. They remain motionless and silent in front of me. I engage them with a series of questions which they dance around with as little effort as they can manage. My attempt to gain information about the where and the why of this moment seems increasingly futile. I now have the unpleasant sensation of my patience beginning to unravel.

Suddenly, emerging from behind the two officials, a diminutive figure appears. He sports a military dress uniform adorned with a collection of merit badges of dubious provenance. The figure also has a thinning shock of close-cropped snow white hair, and a craggy face that has been well-marked by the passage of time.

At first glance I am struck by the air of exaggerated self-importance that the figure is trying ridiculously hard to project. While I continue to absorb this comedic visual a new thought intrudes: the two officials have quietly exited the room. I did not see them leave.

I turn my attention back to *il Duce*. That is what I have chosen to nickname him. My mind is grappling with the search for a plausible explanation for this bizarre apparition. As I am mulling this over, I see that *il Duce* is staring intently at me. Upon confirmation of eye contact, his face slowly morphs into an angry scowl meant to intimidate and instill fear. As his eyes recede behind his protruding brow, he tilts his head at a slightly downward angle for effect. His face has become a mask of pure hostility. Yet, it fails to produce the results that he desires, and in actual fact it reduces *il Duce* to a sad caricature of desperation.

I do not have time for any more of this nonsense. Whatever this may mean, I have decided that I am not interested in discovering it. I renew my search for an exit. After having scanned the entire room again, I am still unable to find a way out. My chest is starting to constrict, the predictable first stop on the road to panic.

Stay calm, breathe, and maintain control I tell myself as I continue my search with increased vigor. It is then that I realize what is not right about this room. It has neither doors nor windows, and yet it still seems very luminous. I have to get out of here.

Silent up until this point, *il Duce* now unleashes a verbal tirade. He is misunderstood. He is the best and everyone wants to be like him. He wants to apologize, and yet feels that he did not do anything that he should have to apologize for. He claims what he did was for the good of all, and that I was the one who benefited the most. I cover my ears with my hands in order to muffle his perverse fabrications and distorted truths.

I begin pacing the room more quickly now, desperately looking for a way out. *Il Duce* is trailing me around the room while squawking incessantly about himself. For some unknown reason I feel that it is critical that I not speak to him or engage him in any way. If I break my silence then I will be acknowledging *il Duce*. I have decided that this is something that I must avoid at all costs.

My avoidance behaviour is the only thing allowing me to cling to some semblance of control in an out-of-control situation. What does all of this mean? The answer, if there is one, is not of critical importance at this moment. I must keep focused to find an escape from this unnerving mixture of confusion and frustration. Once that has been accomplished, then the search for meaning can ensue.

Il Duce is still nattering away like some demented wind-up toy, always just a few steps behind me as he screeches:

"You are the one who benefited the most. You are the one who benefited the most."

Over and over again he repeats this mantra. What the hell is he talking about? How did I benefit? Repetition of propaganda does not create truth. It was evident that *il Duce* had not embraced this concept.

I am sweating profusely. My exertions have gotten me nowhere. How much longer can I keep this up? *Il Duce* must also be tired as he has stopped following me. He has gone quiet and is now seated on a divan at the south end of the great room. As a counterpoint to his silence, he has resumed staring at me again. He is wearing a curious expression. It is unnerving to me so I look away.

Ironically, I find his silence to be more disturbing than his ranting was. I am tempted to break the silence and speak. Instead, I take a seat at the north end of the great room, diagonally opposite him, in order to put the absolute maximum distance between us that the room will allow. A forced compromise I will temporarily accept given that no exit from the room appears to be possible at this moment.

Furtively, I look over to ensure that he is still seated at the other end of the room. He is, and he is still staring at me. I quickly look away and return my attention to finding my way out of my current situation, such that it is. Where did the two officials vanish to? How did they manage to leave this room with no exit?

My train of thought is abruptly interrupted by *il Duce* clearing his throat to get my attention as he says:

"Listen, I need you to..."

I finally explode at this latest intrusion, and angrily cut him off:

"No, you are the one who needs to listen."

These are the first words that I have spoken to him; so much for my vow of silence. I am surprised at my sudden outburst, and chalk it up to pure instinct.

For an instant *il Duce* seems genuinely shocked that I have spoken at all. His shock is solely at the act of my speaking out, with no consideration whatsoever for the content and meaning of what I have said. Dismissively brushing my words aside, he says:

"Come here, I want to show you something." as he stands and motions for me to join him.

I noticed that as he stood up, he also looked up at the ceiling and then down to the floor. He shifted his position a few steps to the left and then looked up again. This unusual behaviour puzzled me. Suddenly, I understood. I had to make a concentrated effort to stifle my laughter when I realized that his movements were for the sole purpose of placing himself in the best light. Interesting, *il Duce* craves the spotlight.

Cautiously I rise up from my seat. *"What do you want to show me?"* There I go, talking again.

Il Duce gives me a beatific smile and replies: *"Come over here and you will see!"*

My options seem very limited at this point. The existing status quo has become rather tiresome. A change, any change has become an attractive proposition to me. I take a few tentative steps towards *il Duce* and then stop to gauge his reaction. His facial expression remains unchanged and his body language presents as unthreatening, even welcoming to a degree.

Still, I do not feel that I can trust him. Yet in spite of that, I cautiously resume my journey towards to him. At this close proximity, I can now see that he is much shorter and much older than he had appeared at a distance.

As my shadow looms over him, he sidesteps it in order to regain his spotlight. I have to suppress the urge to laugh by gently biting my tongue for a few seconds until it passes. In that moment it suddenly dawns on me that I am gaining control of the situation. Perhaps not of the eventual outcome, but at least I now feel in control of my reaction to whatever may arise.

"Ok, I am here. Let's get on with this."

I say in as neutral a tone as possible in order to keep *il Duce* calm and manageable.

Still smiling, *il Duce* leads me to a large oxblood coloured velvet curtain which he sweeps aside with a dramatic flourish to reveal the famous balcony overlooking *Pza. Venezia*. Incredible! How did I miss this? I mull this fresh development over in silence.

Il Duce steps onto the balcony and motions for me to join him. As I cross over the threshold and onto the balcony I can now smell the sweet morning air of the *primavera* and feel the caress of the sun warming my face and hands. It is an incredibly wonderful sensation for me. Unfortunately, it did not last nearly long enough.

It was interrupted when *il Duce* launched into his *acapella* rendition of *Puccini's* aria *Nessum Dorma*. Unsurprisingly, he is unable to compete with the din in the *piazza* below as pedestrians, cars and buses continue on their respective journeys. No one is listening to him. Perhaps no one has ever truly listened to him. This does not seem to register with him on any level. He is in the spotlight and that is all that matters. His delusions sustain his illusions, and vice-versa.

"See, they love me." says il Duce. *"Now let's go for a pizza."*

A sharp explosion on the *terrazzo*...splintering shards of porcelain jolt me awake...the remains of a coffee cup that has just escaped from a nearby table. I am on the terrace of the café at the *Capitolio* with a half-finished espresso in front of me. I have been dreaming.

How long have I been out, I wonder? I dip a finger into the miniature cup; the coffee is ice cold. *Morpheus* is surely laughing at me, wherever he is.

As I gently rub the sleep from my eyes, I turn slightly and direct my gaze across the terrace to the *Pza. Venezia*, and specifically to *il Duce's* balcony. It is empty.

An Unexpected Virtue of Solitude
(Someone Always Leaves)

Another lost weekend; only it is different now. Much different than how it used to be. In the grand scheme of things none of that matters. I have concluded, for the moment at least, that it is simply variations on a theme. Time is a currency that I spend as I wish. There is no carry forward for what remains unspent, and you never know when the store will go out of business.

The *Rooster* doesn't know this. He is stuck in an endless micro-loop of monotony that he cannot recognize, let alone escape from. At his same perch every day, out in front of the train station on the east side of the *Pza. Garibaldi**. Awkwardly strutting a few steps in a random direction, then spinning back and sitting down for a maximum of three seconds. This cycle repeats itself endlessly over the day.

Within this main cycle there exists a smaller one. It occurs on every fifth turn when he stops for a sip of water from a battered paper cup. He growls repeatedly in his purgatory. Over and over again, between his growls, in a near-whisper he softly emits the word *"Poquito"*. How did he wind up here?

The monotony of his obsessive-compulsive behaviour patterns is fraying my nerves. I move away, to a bench where I can no longer hear or see him, and continue to wait for the R2 bus. Its route circles by the

* *See Glossary P. 196*

port, avoiding *via Toledo*, as it winds its way through an office district towards its final stop opposite the *Teatro di San Carlo* and the *Galleria Umberto I*. From there it is a very short walk to the *Gran Caffè Gambrinus*. Over the years I have seen some interesting things on the R2; it is *Napoli* after all.

As I wait, my thoughts drift predictably to her. She will receive them any day now; the gifts that I sent to her. It has been nearly six months since she stopped communicating. Over that time, a level of comfort has emerged in the silence, and the distance that it has put between us.

Paradoxically, that silence may contain elements of fear for both of us. In silence she does not have to face her fear of opening up her life to me; while I simultaneously lean on the silence because I am afraid to close my life to her completely.

The gifts may break her silence...or...they may not. The outcome is unimportant. The course of action chosen was the correct one. Knowing her as I do, I predict that she will be simultaneously pleased and confused by those gifts. She will read into them a myriad of reasons and desires that are simply not there. It is her nature to make the simple complicated, and so she often does this. Sometimes she admits to doing this; on most occasions she does not.

In her apartment she had many prints of lighthouses hanging on the walls. That was years ago...I wonder if they are still there? At first glance those lighthouses struck me as a rather unimaginative subject to build a collection around. One day she confessed to me that one image in particular, the one with waves exploding on the rocks around the lighthouse reminded her of an orgasm. Once she had shared that intimate truth with me, the collection took on a distinctly erotic theme and then its appeal to her became crystal clear.

Yesterday I was very close to the sea, in fact just to the north of a lighthouse as it turned out. I could have easily made my way over the sand and looked for her to the east. In the absence of any longing for her, to do that never even crossed my mind. Once those feelings are gone they never return. That is my truth. She does not want to hear my truth. I believe that she does not even want to hear her truth.

People become adept at lying to themselves in order to avoid their truth. There is a profound sadness in that path. We traveled that path together, her and I, the result of our choices. It did not have to be that way. And yet, there was no other way for it to have concluded this time.

I was left feeling deeply disturbed when I saw her in a way that I could never have imagined. Events that are refracted through different eyes rarely synch up. She had her reality of that evening. The one that I saw was markedly dissimilar. A reconciliation of these divergent realities was improbable, yet not impossible.

In the harsh glare of hindsight, it became obvious that there had been warning signs along the way. The truth which I now had to own was that I had chosen to ignore them. They piled up in a corner;

patiently waiting for their opportunity. Inertia eventually pulled them down upon me. These truths would not be denied their moment. Perfection is illusory. I do the best that I can with that knowledge.

We reached our agreement rather quickly. In fact, she surprised me when, in a brief window of absolute honesty, she revealed her truth to me. In doing so she innocently added a new dimension to her beauty. Did she make this sacrifice in order to protect me? Or, was she simply seeking to protect herself? Whatever her motivation, I cannot help loving her for her honesty in that moment. I wish that she knew this.

The R2 finally arrived. It was half empty; I boarded it and took a seat. A moment later a bag-lady sat down a row in front of me and on the opposite side of the aisle. After she and her many bags had gotten settled, she began eyeballing me. She had those far-away eyes, the kind that had seen too much, and so as a consequence they could no longer see what was right in front of them.

She turned around and glared at me, and then mumbled some gibberish. I was shielded from her hostility by my sunglasses. She could not make eye contact to get a solid read on me. That may just have been the tipping point that set her off. She began shrieking...*Assasino! Assasino!*

In response, I smiled at her. With her eyes locked on mine she resumed her mumblings, then turned away and hit the *Stop Request* button. As the bus slowed, she crab-walked her way down the aisle with her many tattered bags clutched tightly to her chest. She furtively glanced back in my direction every few seconds to see if I was following her. When the bus stopped, and the door opened, she literally flew out of it; running crookedly from her imaginary demons.

Mind shift: it rarely takes very long before I feel like I have been away forever. Not specifically from You or from *Her*; but rather from my life. It defies logic, and yet for whatever reason I find a measure of comfort in it. However, it is never a complete escape. You are still with me. She is also with me; and, so is She... the one before the last.

Remember, I mentioned *Her* to you...the one that was with me for the briefest of moments, until quite unexpectedly She was not. Upon reflection, She never really was with me. She exists on the periphery now, with the others. Footnotes that resurface once they are triggered by random cues, pushing me forcefully back to those memories. Some of the memories are clear and sharp, while others are questionable fragments. How can it be any other way than this?

Still, it was you that entered my consciousness this morning. Thoughts of our next *retrouvaille* came to me as I was preparing to meet the day. I have decided that I very much want to photograph you. To capture your languid eroticism somehow feels important; though I am at a loss to explain why. My desire to have this experience with you leaves me feeling impatient.

In the meantime, I will send you a painting. Actually, it is just a photo of a painting...the *Floating Woman*...swimming in air...limbs akimbo and hair askew. She reminds me of you for some reason. I suspect that sharing this opinion with you might offend you slightly. Perhaps such information would be useful for me to know. For now, I prefer to play on without it.

What comes next is anybody's guess. When you found out that I was writing this book, you coyly asked if there was a place for you in one of the stories. My reply was that if you inspired me, I would write you into a future story. Is that what is happening now? Am I confusing inspiration with infatuation? It would not be the first time. Perhaps, infatuation is the precursor to inspiration. Time will reveal all; if only I can remember to pay attention to it.

Quite randomly, my thoughts suddenly turned to cufflinks. They would be much too formal for my meetings earlier in the day. I would have to explain, not that that matters in the least. The Others are well acquainted with my eccentricities after so many years. In fact, they have come to expect this from me. Disappointing the Others in this regard would also require an explanation. It would seem that regardless of my choices, I will always owe someone somewhere an explanation. Why is it so difficult for them to understand?

It is no secret that you are not Her. You are nothing like Her. Not physically, not intellectually and certainly not spiritually. It must be this way for me. Attempting to replicate the lost with the found is a toxic recipe. Eventually the ghosts rise up in rebellion. I wonder if you know this. More importantly, can you and your ghosts can abide by it?

Isn't that how we have ended up here in the first place? A shift in our respective directions of travel was what put us on a collision course with each other. Very soon now, there must come a time of deeper sharing. Without it, what is between us now is unsustainable. Even with its protection there are still so many ways that this can go sideways. It should not be like that, yet it almost always is.

Why do we blindly distance ourselves from what is sacred? Squandering our precious energies in a mindless quest for trivial satisfactions of fleeting and questionable value? The simple beauty of each moment waits patiently for us to connect with it. How many times did you walk past it today without even seeing it? How about yesterday, or the day before that one? In all of its many forms, beauty is the only true answer.

Fast forward a month or so. As it turned out, you are the *Floating Woman*. Remember, the one from the painting? Floating, or perhaps more accurately drifting through your relationships. From me you will float and drift to your next man, and then to the one after that, and then onto the subsequent ones. This will continue for as long as you keep searching externally for your truth. On some level you must be aware of this?

The R2 reached its terminal stop, opposite the *Teatro di San Carlo* and the few remaining passengers disembarked. I threw a glance ahead and off to my left at the *Pza. del Plebiscito*. Its massive expanse of cobblestones was shiny slick with the light drizzle that was falling. The people crossing through *Plebiscito* were hunched over; protecting themselves from the biting chill of the January wind that was fiercely pushing inland from the Gulf. I moved briskly towards the sanctuary of *Gran Caffé Gambrinus*.

As I walked, I realized that from the outset I had sensed that you and I were a bad pairing. Still, I wanted to give you a reasonable interval of time to reveal yourself. There is no denying that I chose to ignore what my inner voices were whispering to me...about you. Instead, I played along with your game to see where it would lead. Predictably, it did not lead us to a destination of any consequence. However, it did provide a measure of amusement for us to share.

Did you ever have any intention of revealing yourself to me? You seemed to prefer to hide behind your mask of being a riddle without an answer. As I got closer to that answer, the seeds of your fear ripened and you hastily checked out. Following you down your path of fear, or waiting for you to return from it never entered into the equation for me. I was already somewhere else by then. Some pleasant memories of you kept me company as I traveled.

Memories are a strange experience for me now, especially comparing memories with someone else. Specifically, when they share a recollection in vivid detail of an experience they had with me and I draw a total blank on it. As if it never happened. There is no reason to doubt them. Their story is entirely plausible. Then the question to be answered is: where did my memory of that experience go?

I wish that I had more to share with you about that night. The truth is that I simply do not remember more than what I have already told you. It saddens me in a way; how well you can remember that night, and how much I have apparently forgotten about it. Those tiny details of so many memories lived, yet now lost forever in the ether of mind. I know that I was there with you that night. I know this in name only, conceptually with no visual recollection of the details of that event.

A memory arrived, from another night long ago. This one was so pleasant and vivid. You came home with me that night; after our dinner at that bistro that you like so much. You were not physically with me, it was the scent of your perfume that lingered on me... followed me into my bed...where it whispered softly to me...about you.

There are many things that I know with a high degree of certainty. There are also many other things that I know only partially...in fragments. Apparently, you are one of those things. My visceral mystery, tormenting me gently again after decades of calm stillness had passed between us.

Your imprint upon me, both past and present, is a deep one. You are with me again now in such a surreal way that I am caused to question our past lives. If we did not understand it back then, is it any surprise that we still do not understand it now? How many more lives will it be like this between you and I?

Do you remember that one time, so long ago, when for the briefest of moments the curtain was pulled back to reveal a glimpse of our future? What was shown to us was a seductive promise of what we could have been. That moment is forever with us. Yet it is something that we never discuss. Instead, we talk around it, sometimes hinting at it, yet never calling it by name. Our sin of silence cannot cancel out its existence. That moment happened. And yet, there remains other questions that I am afraid to ask you.

While savouring my coffee, I glance around at the cafe's opulent *Art Nouveau* interior, and begin to wonder about the iconic *Belle Epoque* period that played out within these very walls. This does not hold my attention for very long. Clearly, I have some unfinished business with you today.

The memory that comes to me now is of the time when I got lost in the pages of a book that you gave me. I waited for you there. You never made it. I think I know why, but I would still like to hear it from you. Later on, when I set the book aside and closed my eyes, I saw myself walking through a forest. The wind whispering through the trees was the spirits tempting me to join them.

Your words, written and spoken, were similar whispers of seduction. They seemed all too familiar to me. This has always been our pattern together: Seduction, desire, hope and then abandonment. This perverse cycle is sparked by our palpable attraction to one another, fueled by the exhilaration of our imagined potential, and ultimately stalled by the reality of our fears.

Our truth is easy enough to capture. In many ways we are far too much for each other...while in other ways we are nowhere near to being enough for each other. It was during our last conversation that you told me that you did not know what you could give. Ultimately, you chose to give nothing. The simple truth is that nothing is a form of something, and its meaning is clear enough. You never thought to ask me what I needed or wanted. You just decided, and then quickly moved away from me to lie down with your fears.

With that thought I finished my coffee, and took a last look around the cafe. I rose up and swaddled myself with coat, hat and scarf as protection against the elements. It was 6 PM when I exited the *Gran Caffè Gambrinus* and turned left onto *Pza. Trieste e Trento*. The wind had lessened its fury considerably, yet a biting chill remained in the air.

Two blocks south, I made another left onto *via Nardones* and started up the hill towards the apartment. My pace slowed slightly, owing to temptation, as I passed the *Trattoria San Ferdinando*. I would not be stopping in there for a meal tonight. You would already be at the apartment by now, waiting for me to join you.

Last Swim in the Tiber

I had a horrible dream last night. Actually, it was a nightmare. I woke up in a panic, heart pounding and bathed in my own fear sweat. What seems strange to me upon reflection is how I acted in the nightmare.

As it unfolded I seemed to be detached from the outcome, at least initially. My dream state behaviour was in total contrast to my waking behaviour. I was calm in my nightmare, when by all indications I should have been fearful. Conversely, upon waking up in my bed, where I should have felt safe and secure, I momentarily exhibited extreme panic.

In the nightmare, I was forced to endure an unplanned transition of sorts from solid to liquid. *'Oh, I fell into the Tiber *. Let me swim up to the surface and pull myself out and onto the shore.'* I remembered saying this to myself in the dream. I also recalled that the water was bitingly cold and I was sinking. The lights over the *Ponte San Angelo* bridge were shrinking in both size and brightness as they receded from my view. I watched this occur with a bemused fascination, and at one point thought that there was a good photograph to be had here.

Before I fell, I had been walking. *Passeggiata* time in Rome, the best walking city there is! A few hours earlier my walk began with a familiar route that took me northwest to the *Piazza de la Republica*.

*See Glossary P. 196

Via Roma

Even after all these years, and so many visits, it still charms me. I am speaking of the *fontana delle naiadi*, the magnificent fountain by *Rutelli*. An oasis of beauty that dominates the *piazza* in both form and function by forcing the chaotic pulse of Rome to move around her as it makes its way to other corners of the city. Of the multiple sculptures which adorn the fountain, my favorite is the one that I have named Beauty and the Beast. If you have passed by the fountain then I am certain that you know the one I am referring to.

Mostly I favour walks in the *Esquilino* and *Monti* neighbourhoods, but not today. Occasionally, I will cross the tracks and visit *San Lorenzo* to see what the university students are up to. It is inevitable that with each visit I come away from *San Lorenzo* feeling nostalgic. This indulgence leads me to the inescapable conclusion that I am old now. That, in and of itself, is an accomplishment.

In *Esquilino* I can escape the tourist hordes and snatch glimpses of cultures loosely melting together as newcomers establish their foothold in the Eternal City. This process has been ongoing for thousands of years and so the Romans barely notice. At least that is the impression that they appear to give.

It is completely black and silent now. The water is piercingly frigid. I can no longer see the lights or hear the traffic that I know for certain are up there above me. How far down am I? 30 meters? 100 meters? The urge to quantify my situation was still with me. As if somehow putting a number to it could explain everything, and perhaps even point the way to the beginnings of a solution. Not this time. This was the stark reality that I was forced to confront as I continued to sink.

Leaving *Piazza de la Republica* I walked north to reach *Via Veneto*, Not many people know that *Via Veneto* is the best way to get to *Pincio*, but it is not the fastest way. Roma will not reveal her treasures to those who are in a hurry. Did I ever tell you that a friend of mine was a barber on *Via Veneto* in the 1960's, and that Fellini was one of his clients?

I am pleasantly lost now, somewhere in the middle of the *Villa Borghese* grounds. Actually, I am not lost. Pretending to be lost is how I amuse myself whenever I am here. It is very easy to do as the grounds are expansive in their dominance of one of Rome's seven hills. In the middle of the grounds it is very lush, and so incredibly quiet that you can actually forget that you are in the bustling metropolis that is Rome.

On pasts visits to the park I have often taken a spot on the grass and enjoyed listening to the wind singing to the trees. Today, I chose not to linger in the middle and instead decided to press on quickly towards *Pincio*. I stayed in the middle just long enough to bid hello to my old friend and to promise her that I would come back soon for a longer visit.

As I neared *Pincio* I recalled that time when the sky behind St. Peter's became like a painting; an epic canvas of burnt orange and blood red with some golden highlights. A canvas accented by the rich contrast of dark clouds of swallows darting and weaving in unison. On that same day I have memories of another cloud: a group of school-kids riveted on their phones, heads down and thus oblivious to the beauty evolving before them.

Today was not like the one that I just described. Today there were no painted clouds, no swallows, and no kids. It felt colder as the wind picked up its intensity. Down below, in *Pza. Del Poplo* the masses were on the move. It was time for me to abandon *Pincio* and join them.

Did you ever watch your hope get extinguished? I am not talking about your basic hopes that have been repeatedly crushed by the weight of uncaring fate as you navigated your way through life. Not that shiny new bike that you hoped to find under the Christmas tree when you were seven years old. Not the relationship that you deluded yourself into believing would turn into something that it could never have possibly been. Not the promotion at work that you went after full bore but did not get because office politics outweighed merit. No, the hope of which I speak is very different from all of those disappointments.

This form of hope is the eternal flame that resides at the very core of you. It is that inexhaustible spark that pushes you through the heavy mounds of crap that life periodically enjoys dumping on you. It is hardwired into your DNA, and it will not allow you to ever stop trying to overcome. After all, there is always a chance...isn't there?

The hope that stems from that spark is so pervasive that even when you want to give up, it will not let you quit. That is the hope I am speaking of. That was the hope that drifted away from me as I was swallowed up by the river.

I was completely unprepared for this realization of the ultimate loss. It gave rise to sharp feelings of betrayal, and of abandonment as the darkness engulfed me. Honestly, I struggled with this. Simultaneously knowing what it meant on a surface level and yet also having the distinct feeling of not truly being cognizant its deeper meaning. Or was it the reverse of that, with the depth actually being present in the simplicity at the surface? I can tell you that I was never certain of the absolute answer, if in fact there was one.

Before I fell into the *Tiber* I remembered hearing the unmistakable strains of *So What* off *Kind of Blue* escaping from the open window of a car stopped at a traffic light. That particular Miles Davis tune always brought back good memories. The light changed, the car and Miles sped off, and I resumed my walk.

An intrusive thought appeared. Cross the street and take a short cut through *Piazza Navona*. Another thought appeared to me in reply to that first one. At this time of day it will certainly be very crowded. I pushed these thoughts out of my mind and continued along *Lungotevere Tor di Nona* so that I could still follow the river. This route would take me longer but it saved me from having to endure the crowds.

It was not very long after I had made that choice when I realized that

I was going to die. Not in the typical way. I mean we all know of our pending mortality on some level or other, and we either make peace with it or ignore it. What I am talking about here is feeling Death's cold whisper in my ear...right then! Obviously, that was a first for me. Can I be completely honest with you? I accepted this event better than I had imagined that I would. At this stage of the game it felt like liberation to me.

Before I had made the choice to follow the river, I recall trying to decide what to do when I reached *Ponte Garibaldi*. Cross over the bridge and into *Trastevere*, or continue along *Lungotevere di Cenci* and wind up in *Testaccio?*

I opted to avoid making this choice until I reached the *Ponte Garibaldi*. If you take a moment to think about it the conclusion is inescapable. Your today is perpetually spilling over into your tomorrow. Only, not this particular time. I never made it to that bridge and so that choice got postponed forever as it turned out.

Leaving *Pincio* had been the right decision. It was the golden hour now. The time of day when the sun gently wrapped Rome in her embrace and the city responded with a visible glow. Visiting Rome in November has always been my preference. The light is incredible for photography at this time of year. I felt a tingle of excitement as I retrieved my camera from my backpack. I was certain that Rome would reward me with an iconic image today.

Exponential gravity was in play as the eternal waters of the *Tiber* gripped me in their embrace. They saturated my clothing, and found a home in my boots and my backpack. They pulled me down ever faster into the inky blackness.

Unable to accept the frigid water, my muscles knotted up in paralysis, and my body adopted a calm resignation to its fate. What choice did it have? I noticed that I did not feel cold any longer, just increasingly numb. Only moments ago I was walking. Now I am sinking. It requires much less effort. This I can tell you with absolute certainty.

I can no longer see anything in the blackness so I just shut my eyes and try to look within. Time seems to be suspended and I am feeling serene. Instinctively, I know that I do not have enough time left to contemplate what I have never seen, nor what I have seen but will never see again. My understanding of the situation is that what is in motion now will be absolute in its finality. There is no way back, this time around.

They say that it can be a matter of inches between life and death. They say a lot of things. Today they were right; it was a matter of inches. I like to think that time also plays a significant part in the equation. They do not say much about time except *tempus fugit*, and some nonsense about stitches and saving nine. There is also the currently fashionable wisdom on how one should live in the present moment because that is all we truly have. I remain unconvinced as to the veracity of said wisdom. I prefer to take satisfaction from the past, and to have anticipation for the future.

Those inches and moments are certainly of consequence. Yet they are merely facilitators after fate has already decided. One's fate is determined by one's choices. My fate was decided by my choice to follow the *Tiber* and not to go through *Piazza Navona*. Falling into the *Tiber* could only have occurred based upon that choice. This same result was not possible in *Piazza Navona*. Choices are inextricably linked to fate.

There was nothing at all for a period. No sensation of body. No conscious thought. Then at some point there was light. It was very dim at first. Recognition of the presence of this light was soon followed by the sensation that I was being gently pulled towards it.

Then the light seemed to grow brighter. An awareness that the light was gradually replacing the darkness dawned on me. This transformation mirrored elements of the photographic process. That was the last thought that struck me. I wonder if we can agree, you and I, that in some measure, the light and the darkness pervade all aspects of life?

Carnival Masks

Have you ever seen Wes Anderson's film *The Darjeeling Limited*? It is about masks in an obviously subtle way. The masks are worn by three estranged brothers; during their various misadventures on a train journey through India. Even their mother is wearing a mask when they finally meet her.

Truth be told, we all wear masks; even when we are alone with ourselves. You might even be wearing one right now as you read this? Picking up masks and learning to wear them begins early in life for most of us. It starts out as a child's game, yet over time it becomes an unfortunate accessory for survival in daily life. Some people are very comfortable with their masks, while others never seem to be truly at ease in them.

As children we quickly come to understand that these masks can often get us what we desire. It is the outcome that is our sole focus. We are too young to understand the complexities of intent, as well as why the masks have power that they do. That knowledge comes much later; and even then only for some of us. By that point we wear our masks in most situations, if not all of the time. Most people will never admit to doing so.

Over the years you have probably collected a variety of masks for different situations. Most people have, so I do not see how you could be any different. Are you comfortable behind your masks? That is what I am most curious about.

We all have our reasons for wearing our masks. We may feel that our reasons are unique and that they are perfectly rational. The simple truth is that upon closer examination our reasons typically reveal themselves to be irrational and quite common.

We like to believe that our masks protect us. In actual fact, our masks are more often instigators who cause us and others all sorts of misfortunes and misunderstandings. What if I shared with you the notion that your masks perpetuate a false security that blinds you to reality, such that it is? Anyhow, that is enough about the masks for now. We will return to them a little later on. I promise.

I will confess to you that I prefer to travel by train whenever possible. It is much more civilized than air travel, in my opinion. Some trains are now faster than air travel up to a certain distance. Faster isn't always better though.

When time permits, for me the choice is obvious. I enjoy the slow trains, the *Regionales** that stop in each little town or village along the way. The scenery is better and the people are more interesting on the slow trains. I have always found this to be true, especially in Italy.

My favorite train ride originates in *Ventimiglia*. It is the first town in Italy that you arrive at after crossing the border from France. There are

See Glossary P. 198

both fast trains and slow trains leaving from there. I take the slow ones when my schedule permits, which is often these days. My destination is always Rome now. In the past, it was *Napoli* for several years, but prior to that it was Rome.

This train route hugs the coastline. Initially, it follows the *Ligurian Sea* and then makes a sweeping right that begins more or less at *Genoa* and ends at *Livorno*. That leg of the journey takes up the better part of a day. I typically overnight in the *Cinque Terre*, usually in *Vernazza* where there is a B & B that I favour with rooms overlooking the main *piazza* and the sea. Sometimes, I stay for two or even three nights; but not on this particular trip.

The charm of the slow trains is in large part owing to all of the stops that they make along the way. Sometimes, once you have gotten off the train, you feel a very compelling urge to stay in a place. If that seduction occurs and you decide to stay, rest assured that the train will continue on without you.

More often though, a stronger urge pulls you away and you get back on the train. Usually, it starts with a small tingle of uncertainty and ends with feelings that are a contradictory mixture of regret and anticipation. Regret at leaving this stop, yet anticipation to see what the next stop will bring. Of course these feelings, how they resonate, and how long they last are different for each of us. I hope that this rather simplistic explanation will suffice for you.

Over the course of my rail journeys I have witnessed many passengers who abandoned their travels and settled on a particular stop. I still wonder how they are able to do that, and why I am unable to do the same even after all these years.

I distinctly recall the period when I came to a realization; and of how it arrived wrapped up in a question. Initially, it was as a result of the train being unnaturally empty. At least that was how it appeared to me. As I walked through the other cars I did see a few other people. However, they did not acknowledge me; preferring instead to peer out the windows at the ever changing landscape. I assumed that they were also going to Rome.

Later on in the journey, the question of uncertainty began to haunt me. I couldn't put it down to a specific day or a specific stop, but something had definitely changed. The train had started to fill up again, and I recognized many of the recent additions from previous journeys that we had shared in the past. At first they seemed friendly enough. Some of them even recognized me. Even so, it somehow felt unnatural and a bit contrived to me.

It was then that I began to consider the notion that people never truly get past their uncertainty. I think they simply make considerable efforts to attempt to bury it. Yet, in spite of their efforts, every so often their uncertainty resurfaces. When this happens, they have to heap more dirt on it and tamp it back down. Sometimes their uncertainty becomes too strong; as if their shovel had broken, or they had run out of dirt.

Once their uncertainty has gained the upper hand it begins to consume them. This is the point when people should leave that particular place and get back on the train. However, most people never see this as it is happening. That is likely because the changes are incredibly subtle; they unfold in minute increments that are barely perceptible. The darker side of this equation is that no one wants to admit to it, even if they do see sporadic flashes of the truth. It is far easier to hide behind a mask, and so that is what most people do.

As I am sure you know from experience the place is very welcoming at first, seductive with opportunities and promises. In the beginning the place is always very giving and asks for little if anything in return. Yet, that never lasts. How could it possibly last? The bill always comes due.

The realization occurs at different times for everyone. It is the moment when they see that the place they chose to stop at is not what they thought that it was. It is in that precise moment they begin to understand that the place has slowly taken from them far more than it has given to them. It is in that specific moment that they can no longer recognize themselves, as they now see only a faded spectre of who they once were. That is the exact moment when they must decide if they are strong enough to get back on the train and try to salvage what still remains of them.

For most people it is too late. Getting back on the train solves nothing. They have lost too much of themselves; and they have brought the place aboard the train with them. They are contaminated. The place, and their history with it, now travels with them like a disease to their next destination.

I myself had pretty much given up disembarking at the stops a while back. There no longer seemed to be much point to it. In fact I cannot recall that last time that I did; or even when I last felt the compelling urge to do so. I guess it stopped being important for me at some point, for reasons that I choose to no longer remember.

In order to replace what I no longer cared about, I developed a keen interest in who was getting on the train at each stop. It quickly became apparent to me that there was something different about these folks. We were on the same train yet it seemed to me that we were on vastly different journeys.

The thing that really intrigued me about them was that distracted look that they had behind their masks. Their far away eyes. They were gazing back into the past; either desperately looking for something that they had left behind, or else nervously scanning to see what was gaining on them. Damaged goods I thought to myself; broken shovels and no more dirt left.

Over time the train became very full. We were still quite a distance from Rome. As the train filled up it got harder to keep track of people, and so I shifted my focus in a new direction. This was infinitely more challenging as it required significant measures of subtlety, tact and planning in order to produce the desired results.

My first several attempts ended in disaster. In retrospect, this was not the least bit surprising. I struggled to determine if it was my approach, or if it was the unapproachability of my targets. I even considered abandoning this pastime entirely and switching to an easier one. In the end I decided that it was a bit of both, and from there I worked to refine my methods and to select my targets with greater care.

At the outset, I was content to just study them and their interactions from a reasonable distance. Over time I ventured closer. It took me a long time to see it, because it was so understated. Hidden really; until I had learned where and how to look for it. Then it became very easy to spot.

What I observed is difficult for me to capture authentically with words. I ran through an infinite number of possibilities of how to most accurately describe this to you. Finally, I chose what I felt was the one that best illustrated the truth I had discovered. That is the one that I am going to share with you now.

The streets of Havana, the capitol of Cuba, are filled with private communal taxis called *Almendrones*. I only mention the *Almendrones* because there is a parallel between these old heaps and the passengers on the train. An *Almendron*, literally slang for a big almond, is pre – 1959 American iron. Keeping these cars on the road for 60 plus years has required significant amounts of ingenuity and adaptability. Rumour has it that the aging transmissions of many of the *Almendrones* have been Frankenstein-ed with Russian tractor gears among other misfit parts. Watching and hearing these *Alemdrones* as they lurch through the streets of Havana serves to confirm the rumours.

Based on what I had observed, the people on the train were just like the *Almendrones*. Over the course of their lifetimes they have also broken down and have wound up with tractor gears and other misfits with some teeth shorn off. As a result they still managed to function, but only sub-optimally and most times not for very long. This was something that I had seen again and again on board this train; people who seemed to become frozen as soon as their pasts intruded upon their present.

Initially, I observed that their willingness to try again seemed to be genuine. It was clear that they wanted to get off this train and find a place to call home. They seemed to be sincere about moving forward and trying to build a future again. They spoke most of the right words and did most of the right things in preparation for this.

However, it never lasted for very long. How could it once their pasts caught up to them? Once their masks slipped, their shovels broke, or the dirt ran out. That was when their gears started to grind, some more teeth got shorn off, and they eventually just seized up.

After a time this became very difficult for me to watch. I wanted so badly to reach out to them. Instinctively, I knew that they did not want me to...and that ultimately...there was no value to be achieved in my doing so.

The worst part for me was seeing their vanishing glance. It only lasted for a millisecond yet that glance spilled out all of their guilt and shame, and put it on display. It was as if their tattered carnival masks could no longer cover up what they did not want the world to see. In that briefest space in time they knew that I knew that they were exposed. After that had transpired, it could never be the same between us.

Their vanishing glance disappeared as soon as they averted their eyes; and I felt immensely relieved when they did. At that point most of them usually fidgeted with what was left of their mask in a futile attempt at increasing its protective coverage. From there they stubbornly carried on as if everything was normal. We all knew that normal had been impossible since well before they had gotten back on board the train. However, no one had the courage to approach this taboo.

I could no longer speak with them once I had seen their vanishing glance; it made me too sad. Fortunately, it seemed that they did not want to speak to me either. The ones who dared to look back in my direction, after all of that, now had the far away eyes.

All of that caused me to wonder about people, about this thing that we like to call *Self*, and about how human interactions impact both people and *Self*. After all of the questions and answers I tossed around I was left with one that I could not answer: At what point does a person realize that they no longer recognize who they are?

My best guess was that the only way to even begin to know this would be to somehow keep score. Yet we are told repeatedly that we should never keep score. It is the people who tell you not to do this that turn out to be the ones who are doing exactly this behind your back. It is a good time to get back on the train when you discover that the people around you have been keeping score.

An unfamiliar feeling had been building up inside of me for a while now. After considerable rumination I arrived at the conclusion that there was little, if anything at all, left for me on that train. Those people with their tattered carnival masks were no longer of any interest to me.

How long should I search for something that can never be found? After years of riding the trains I had become convinced that I would never find the stop where I would want to stay. It felt as if I could no longer stay on this train, but that I could not disembark from it either. I was caught up in a bizarre paradox. Feeling paralyzed by the realization that a choice between two equally unappealing choices was in reality no choice at all. To me, it felt distinctly like a forced compromise. Or maybe it was simply defeat? Attrition wins out eventually, it plays the long game and its patience is always rewarded.

Not very long after that, the day arrived when I took a decisive course of action. I made my choice. I stepped off that train with the notion that this time it was forever. There was no compelling reason behind this decision that I can share with you. Maybe I was simply tired of my long journey? What I can tell you with absolute certainty is that I felt a disconcerting lack of conviction about my choice. That feeling left me less than optimistic about my chances of success.

Still, the die was cast as Caesar was reported to have said as he and his legions crossed the *Rubicon* in 49 B.C. He had also decided to visit Rome, so we had this in common. History recorded that he reached his destination. I will not reach mine. I thought that you should know this.

The air was heavy with the oppressive summer heat of midday. As I followed the cracked and sun-bleached concrete platform to the main station, something made me pause. I turned back to the train and caught sight of my carnival mask lying on the floor of the train car vestibule. Then the door closed and it vanished from my sight.

As the train slowly departed from the station; I recall thinking that I no longer needed it anyway. Which one: the tattered mask, or the train? The answer that struck me was both.

Inside the station, I set my suitcase down beside a sink in the Men's room. The sink was the last one in the row and it had a wall running perpendicular to it. Still, as was my habit, I kept one foot pressing the suitcase to the wall. You can never be too careful they say. Besides, old reflexes die hard. That is another thing that they say.

I cranked the cold tap to the right and then cupped my hands under the faucet to collect some water. I splashed it on my face; it felt all fresh and alive. I did that three more times.

It always made me feel better about things; the cool water not the repetition. Then I looked up from the sink and into the mirror. My reflection looked back at me with the far away eyes. At least I was still in Italy, I thought as I reached down for my suitcase.

Someone Always Leaves – II & III

My first glimpse of her was in a photo where she stood with two other women. The photo was part of a memory collage of a hundred or so snapshots that occupied a wall in a friend's country house in Campania*. A rich visual history of the many good times that originated at that house.

This photo stood out from the rest; and she stood out from the other two women in the photo. My friend who owned the house noticed me lingering. She sidled up and asked me point-blank, "See something interesting?" I have always admired and appreciated her directness. A few days later, my friend provided me with a phone number and an invitation to call the woman in the photo.

Several years later, on a visit to that same house, my friend offered to take this particular photo off the wall because she knew it made me sad. I told her to leave it up because it only made me a little sad. I had lost something that was very precious to me. It is not accurate to say that I lost it. The actual truth is that it was taken from me.

We had our first date at a little café overlooking the Tiber. She was forgivably late. I had pretty much expected that, traffic and parking challenges in Rome you see. Our unfamiliarity with each other rapidly faded, and we settled into a nice conversational groove. The hours flew

See Glossary P. 198

by and we were interrupted by closing time. I walked her to her car and we agreed to meet again soon.

She lived on the periphery, with her parents. This was temporary, to save on expenses, as she had recently finished her studies and was now in the job hunt. It did not even register as a potential problem, why would it have?

We began spending more and more time together. There were long lazy days and nights enjoying the Centro and each other. Is there a better place than Rome to fall in love? In this specific instance the answer was no; there was no better place.

Her parents became curious. A dinner invitation was proffered, and accepted. It did not go well. I arrived late due to traffic, and apparently I stayed too long. I never saw them again. In fact, they refused multiple requests to meet with me a second time.

What I did not see that night, and only came to understand later, was that this had not been a normal dinner with a normal family. Looking back on it now, it was more like an interview disguised as a dinner. It was their chance to gather as much information about me as they could. Later, they selectively distorted bits of that information in order to fulfill their agenda.

Truth be told, I am too trusting and am often more forthcoming with information than I should be. The harsh reality is that there are people who want to learn all that they can about you for the sole purpose of turning it against you in the future. This is a lesson that I have still not managed to take to heart, despite the several opportunities that I have had to do so.

Some people feign interest in you in order to feel superior, and thus better about who they are. Others fear what is beautiful, what they do not have themselves, or what they do not understand. In reaction to their fears, their default response is to seek to destroy beauty in order to preserve their flawed status quo.

Those are very simplistic theories, I will admit. Sometimes it is far more complex than it appears to be on the surface. Other times though, it is not complicated at all. People often make it far more complicated than it needs to be. That is an environment where drama flourishes.

She also thought the dinner had gone well and so had clearly missed the underlying motivations that were in play. What she was subjected to the next morning by her family meant that Rome was never the same for us again. Even though we tried to ignore it, the unspoken was always lurking in the background. Our nights together with Rome had once seemed endless and full of promise. Now they were truncated by her fear: "It's getting late. I had better go..." had become her mantra.

At that time we were both in a period of our lives where we were finding our way. Then we found each other, and felt that we could find our way together. Others apparently thought much differently.

Others thought, and made considerable efforts to claim that our relationship was impeding our individual progress. It was hardcore gaslighting, and it was hidden behind a brittle veneer masking an ugly truth: a toxic need for control. That was what ultimately hijacked our love.

Over a period of a few weeks I watched her gradually slip away from me and retreat deeper into herself. When we were together I could sense her mentally calculating if a few hours with me were worth the drama that she would return home to face.

Initially, we spoke about it at length. We racked our brains trying to find a solution. We failed to do so, and soon we grew tired of this unsolvable puzzle. Sadly, we found ourselves in agreement that our present reality had too many obstacles to overcome.

And so we both left.

After an interlude, part III arrived very unexpectedly. When I reflect on it, even after all this time, I am still surprised at how our paths managed to cross again. At that moment both of our circumstances, hers in particular, had changed dramatically. Based upon the powerful symmetry present in our initial time together, how could we pass up the chance to explore it further?

A couple of years had passed since our first encounter. Our sporadic emails had completely died out several months back. Suddenly, one day out of the blue a note arrived. My response to it precipitated a phone call from her. That call did not produce her desired result. She immediately called me again and a meet-up was arranged.

When we met for coffee, close to Termini one afternoon, she was all wide-eyed, nervous, and unable to speak her feelings. It seemed to me that very little had changed with her. In a sense it was perfectly understandable. Expressing her feelings was something she had always struggled with since I had known her. In the past, within the safety of our relationship, she had made great strides on this. At that precise moment we did not have a relationship. That left her exposed and struggling for traction on the high-wire without a net.

I should have cut my losses right there and walked out. Fortunately, I did not. I left the door open a crack and invited her to walk through it. She did. What transpired as a result took us on a fantastic journey to places that we had never visited before. True confessions; I have never found my way back to many of those places since. Of course, it goes without saying that I cannot speak for her in this regard.

How can I best describe it to you? Well, I can start off by telling you that there are specific memories that stand out as being more exceptional than the others. Yet, at the same time you should also know that even the minutiae contributed. In essence it was a continuum of love, with each aspect of our time together being necessary to the existence of the whole. Upon reflection, I believe that everything we shared were like pieces of a puzzle that just naturally clicked into place.

Others saw it. How could they not? One night we were enjoying the sunset at Pincio when a tourist spontaneously approached us and said: "You two make a very beautiful couple. I can see you are very much in love." This had never happened to me, before that day. It has never happened since that day. Her words were an expression of pureness and simplicity, and yet they also had a measure of depth to them.

Elle told me that she loved me one day. She followed her declaration with a magnificent kiss, and then her confession that I was the first man that she had ever said this to. She told me that it was because she had never been sure if she had been in love or not.

I felt two profound emotions in that moment. I was elated to hear her declaration of love. Simultaneously, I was sad for her that she had been denied this experience until now; simply because she was the one who had denied herself this.

She was a water spirit, of that I am certain. We spent a lot of time together by the water. We took long walks and many coffees along the Tiber. We also spent days enjoying the sea at the lido in Ostia as often as we could. She was closer to her self by the water. She just seemed more at peace and content there than she did back in the city. She generously led me down the path of tranquility with her on those times by the water.

I distinctly recall how words became intrusive, and of how economical with our speech we became during those water moments. There is a simple elegance in silence, especially when it is shared. I have never been this quiet and this comfortable in silence with anyone since. Over the years, I have learned to be very comfortable with silence when I am alone.

We enjoyed a year of magic together. Then we endured four months of brutality, under attack by her parents once again. We struggled to get back to the place where the magic was. We never did find our way back there. It seemed beyond tragic that something so pure and beautiful was destroyed by fear and ignorance. You can take the peasant out of the village, but you can't take the village out of the peasant; as the old saying goes.

To this day it still surprises me when I encounter people who let their irrational fears suppress all logic. For them fear is an easy and comfortable default response, while logic appears to be mysterious and requiring significant effort. Acting on the basis of irrational fears is a symptom of a diseased ego.

People like this do not see any value in compromise. They cannot be reasoned with, as they have no use for facts that contradict their distorted truths. Arguing with these people is akin to wrestling with a pig, someone once told me. The predictable outcome is that the pig has a great time and you wind up covered in pig excrement and mud!

Although I profess to know better, every so often I opt to join the pigs in their pen. I am choosing to allow myself the flawed belief that this time the outcome will be different. It never is. I always wind up covered in mud and pig shit. No matter, I know that I can exit the pen at any time I want and they cannot. I know that I can easily get clean again, and that they cannot.

Their ego has them on a very tight leash and confined to a dark world of ignorance, fear and anger whenever they encounter the truth. It is a world that few of them ever escape from because they are unable to recognize where they are. Thus they are unable to conceive of the need for and the existence of an exit from their darkness.

It was glaringly obvious that they inhabited different worlds. The contrast between them was so vivid. One was clearly crippled by her selfishness, and yet had deluded herself into believing that she was winning in life. The other had adapted to years of abuse living under the first one's overbearing shadow. Yet somehow she had cultivated a pure heart filled with love, hope, and passion for life in her own quiet way.

I thought that this time around she was strong enough to finally break free from her shackles. I thought that our year together had provided her with the doorway to a beautiful future. It turned out that I was wrong once again. Of course, I cannot appreciate what it felt like for her to be forced to confront the ugliest of ultimatums.

And so she left, again.

Many years have passed now. Predictably, the memories of our time together have faded considerably. There is a path back to those vanishing memories. It is in the letters and cards that she wrote to me. Initially, after she left, I recall poring over her letters searching for answers as to why things ended. There were no answers to be found in those pages, and so I stopped looking for them.

The letters were left to sleep for a lengthy period. When I eventually chanced upon them, I realized that my focus had shifted from seeking answers to enjoying the memories that those letters could rekindle. It had become about honouring what was a very special time, and about appreciating the fact that there was still pleasure in revisiting it occasionally. It goes without saying that my focus is very selective on those visits. I have chosen to remember what was beautiful. More importantly, I have chosen to forget how that beauty was taken from me.

As special as it was, it is an unassailable fact that that particular time now inhabits the distant periphery of my memory. Like a book stored in a bookcase that I pass by every so often, yet never really see among all the other books. I have to make a special effort to find that book, and to take it from the shelf. Then, once it is in my hands, I need to close my eyes and think back to when I first read it and to what it meant to me at that time.

Until today, sharing this with you now, I do not recall the last time I made that effort. Still, I stubbornly want to cling to the belief that memories can stay with you forever if you read them in the right way. Honestly, I must confess that it takes me longer to find my way back to those memories now than it used to. I expect that one day I will be unable to find my way back to them at all.

Tossing Coins

I am very tired. My back aches, my ass is numb, my legs are stiff, and my feet are swollen. This is getting harder on my body every time I do it. Why do I subject myself to this? Why does anyone for that matter? For the moment I am still of the mind that the benefits continue to outweigh the costs. I do not know how much longer I will be able to sustain this opinion. Yet, it is this opinion that is essential to my convincing myself to keep doing it.

We have been descending for a while now, so the sea is closer and is showing increasing detail. Moments later I see land and I immediately feel better. The crisp light of a new day and the verdant greenery that leads from the coastline to the tarmac is the welcome I have come to expect from the *primavera**. This welcome makes me feel at home, even though this is not my true home. I was not born here, at least not in this particular life. I do not reside here, not yet in any case though I am hopeful for the future.

The plane does what planes must always do; trading the graceful freedom of sky for the clumsy constraints of *terra firma*. *Fiumicino*...back to *Fiumicino* once again. I can't help smiling at this thought, and yet I detest airports and hate flying in general.

There was a time when air travel used to be an exotic adventure, before the fallout from 9/11. Then the bean counters took control,

*See Glossary P.199

advising their masters to cram in more seats per plane, and to charge for every little thing. There was a time. Yes, there was a time and it was not so very long ago.

The seatbelt light goes off and the mad scramble ensues at the overhead bins. And then the pushing starts, always with the pushing. People still seem unable to grasp the concept that until the door opens to the gangway there is nowhere for them or anyone else to go. When we do finally start to move, we look like a procession of penguins as we stiffly sway and hobble down the narrow cabin aisle with our over-stuffed carry-ons.

Once inside the terminal, the crowd heads left to the luggage carousels while I veer to the right with my fingers crossed. Why are my fingers crossed? Well, it is because I am hoping that they are still there. Another few steps, another right turn leading me into the hallway and...there they are...the bank ATM and the *Leonardo da Vinci Shuttle* ticket machines. Ninety seconds later, my first ritual is completed and I am headed back to join the others at the baggage carousel. I now have 500 Euros in my left front pocket and a shuttle ticket in my right back pocket.

Now with luggage in tow, I stride towards the escalator that will bring me to the station platform. It is cruel I know. I sort of scold myself for doing it, and yet I can't help enjoying it. I am talking about the self-satisfied smirk I wear as I walk past the queue at the currency exchange.

These are the same people who were on my plane. The same people who twenty minutes from now will be lining up again at the kiosk to buy their shuttle tickets. The same people who will finally be boarding the shuttle at *Fiumicino* while I am already in the *Centro* enjoying my first espresso of this trip. I frequent that little café just across the street from the west entrance of *Termini*. It is a fantastic location for people watching.

The inescapable irony, for me at least, is that these are the same people who literally trampled each other to get off the plane so that they could then wait in the lines for currency and shuttle tickets. I also waited in lines, once. That was many years ago on my first visit to Rome. That was before the rituals were born.

Question: what is your opinion of rituals? I find them to be useful for a variety of reasons. For the most part it is because they save me time and energy by making pedestrian tasks quick and painless. My efficiency rituals are the by-product of many travel adventures. The rituals are guided by *kaizen*; evolving as necessary to meet the circumstances that they are faced with.

I do not buy into the superstitious preventative type of rituals. I have no use for them, even though I know them to be sacred to many folks scattered around the globe.

Truth be told, I do permit myself a single exception where superstitious rituals are concerned. Let me tell you a bit about that. To begin with I suppose that we can chalk it up to my thirty year infatuation with *Bella Roma,* a truly exceptional city, the Eternal City!

Honestly, I have lost count of the number of times I have done it. My best guess would be that it is correlated to the number of visits I have made here. Well not exactly, it would be minus one because I was not acquainted with this ritual on my first visit.

As a confession of sorts I will share with you that it is not in my nature to be superstitious. I feel that it is important for you to know that. In fact, you should be aware that I am a devotee of logic and reason. The explanation is pretty simple. It is because these are the things that I apply on a daily basis in my professional life. Predictably, these traits have spilled over into my private life.

Still, I am of the mind that one can indulge in the occasional exception. I trust that you will agree that making exceptions every so often is absolutely necessary in order to keep life interesting.

My exception, my specific ritual, always begins in the same manner: fishing around deep inside my left front pocket to find a one euro coin. It still feels awkward to me for some reason, these euros, when I used to toss *Lire.* I guess there are some things I will never get fully accustomed to. Ultimately, it does not seem to matter since the result they produce has been the same so far.

As the years have piled up I have come to realize that I place more significance on past events than I used to. The past is solid and tangible to me. Since I have lived it, the past is familiar and comforting to me. I barely trust the present, and I have little if any confidence in the future based on what I observe around me these days. We live in degenerate times was an assessment once offered to me by a Buddhist Monk. I find myself to be in complete agreement with him. In fact more so with every day that passes.

Once my fingers have extracted the coin they then hold it aloft briefly. Just long enough for me to whisper to it *"Bring me back to Bella Roma."* before I turn my back on the *Trevi* and toss the coin in a high arc over my left shoulder.

After I hear the plonk, as my coin breaks the water, I am content in the knowledge that my return to Rome is now guaranteed. After all, this quirky legend has brought me back to Rome time after time so there must be some substance to it. At least that is what I choose to believe.

On most of my visits to the *Trevi* fountain I like to reminisce about my first time. My introduction to this little ritual occurred during a night on the town with my friends Luca and Simone. They are brothers and they have adopted me as their third brother. Our bond of friendship has grown from the many adventures we have shared in Rome over the years.

Today I am alone at the *Trevi*. Actually, that statement is less than accurate. I am currently sharing the *Trevi* with a few hundred other folks. It is the brothers who are missing today...my brothers.

The large crowd that currently surrounds the *Trevi* produces a constant hum of murmurs that is occasionally punctuated by the excited shriek of a child. I want to block out this white noise in order to be closer to my thoughts. I move right down to the fountain and take a seat on its edge. Now the hum is masked by the rush of the water cascading over the ornate marble sculptures. It feels much cooler here, in the open space right by the water.

Apparently, the fountain gets turned off every night for a hour or so when city workers collect all the coins. I remember reading somewhere, or maybe it was someone who knew about these things that told me, that the daily collection averages around 3,000 euros. Apparently, that money finds its way to local charities. I have never seen the *Trevi* shut off and dry. I make a mental note to try and observe this phenomenon one night.

The sound of the water causes me to get lost in my memories; taking me all the way back to the first visit to Rome in September of 1987. I did not visit the *Trevi* on that trip and so I did not toss a coin into it. Yet, somehow I managed to make my way back to Rome in 1989 which more or less invalidates the main premise behind the coin tossing ritual. Where the *Trevi* is concerned I have chosen to suspend logic, and instead believe that this is simply one of life's many mysteries that need not be explained.

The elegance, beauty and harmony of *Niccola Salvi's* design leave me in awe every time I am blessed to gaze upon it. On each visit to the *Trevi* I see something new that I do not recall seeing before. With every successive visit my appreciation of this masterpiece grows.

As a consequence of this deepening appreciation, the importance of the coin toss has become amplified. I must return here. To not return to Rome is not an option. And so, I make any and all efforts necessary to ensure my return. To not toss a coin is not an option. I must toss a coin. And so, I always toss a coin.

Sometimes I perform this ritual immediately once I arrive at the *Trevi*. Other times, after I have hung around awhile, I do it as I am leaving. Sometimes I do it the day after I arrive in Rome, and other times I leave this ritual until the day just before I leave.

There is one constant to my ritual. Each time that I do it I stand in a different spot and try to aim for an area where I have not tossed a coin before. Honestly, I do not know why I have added in this extra step; a small ritual wrapped within a larger ritual. I guess that is just the way that it has evolved over time. I am descending further down into the rabbit hole of superstitions. So far it has been a pleasant trip.

In the quiet hours of a new day, before the dawn breaks, is the best time to visit. The *Trevi* is much different in the night, once the tourists have gone to bed. At that time I can't help but imagine the famous scene in *La Dolce Vita* when Anita Ekberg beckoned Marcello

Mastroianni to join her in the fountain. Sometimes, when I am feeling Rome-sick, I play that movie so that I can feel closer to Rome even though I am far away from her.

There was a time when I actively pursued acquiring an apartment in Rome. I thought that I had had it all figured out. Rent it out over the high season from May through September, and take the remaining months for myself. I had even interviewed property managers and looked into mortgage financing. That dream died with the adoption of the euro which caused apartment prices to more or less double, and so my numbers no longer came close to making any sense.

A few years later the dream came alive again for a brief instant but quickly evaporated when it became clear that the price to be paid was far too high. There was no money in the equation this time. No, this time the price was marriage. The offer of a life in Rome in a posh apartment near *Campo di Fiori* was made far too early by a woman whom I had become involved with. The offer had an air of desperation about it, and the manner in which it was presented smelled like bribery.

Her chosen mask was a studied affectation of radical chic. For her, dating me was predominantly about her image. I was a new accessory of foreign pedigree that she could leverage to appear stylish and trendy for this season. A future based on the whims of fashion seemed to be a very tenuous one to me.

Inevitably, I came to see her as a unicorn. Her family's financial means had made her the quintessential poor little rich girl. The irony in play was that owing to her birthright her survival was a certainty. Yet as a consequence, she lacked the skill-set necessary for true survival on her own in the real world. The conclusion was obvious; we could not work for a sustainable period on any level that I could identify.

Brushing aside the intrusion of those memories I returned to the present and reviewed how I came to be at the fountain today. In a sense it was opportunistic. What struck me was the obvious deviation from my established pattern. I had clearly 'coloured outside the lines'. In the absence of a predictable pattern, can you still consider it to be a ritual?

Here is how it happened. Arriving at *via del Corso*, I glanced at my watch and noted that I had time to spare before my evening appointment. Since I had the time, and was fairly close by, why not do it now? Well, first of all this would be different because I am at the middle point of my trip, as opposed to at the start or the end of it. That shouldn't make any difference, should it?

I decided that it would not make any difference as I crossed over *via del Corso* and made a right, and then a couple of blocks south I made a left. I heard the crowd just before I could see it. Conversely, I saw the water before I heard it. The sublime paradox of those two experiences was not lost on me.

As I made my way to the fountain I reached into my pocket for a coin. It was way too soon. Why was I in such a hurry to get this over and done with? I did not have an answer. I released the coin and withdrew my hand from my pocket. I will know when it is the right time.

I had been seated on the edge of the fountain for about twenty minutes. Why am I thinking when I should be observing? Glancing at my watch confirms yet again that there is no rush. I relaxed and turned to gaze upon the fountain. I said hello to my old friends there, and then began to look for new ones that I have not met on prior visits. There are no longer any, I have met them all.

It is the right time now. The time for the ritual. Retrieving a coin from my pocket, I hold it aloft briefly just as I have so many times in the past. I lean in and softly whisper to the coin: *"Bring me back to Bella Roma"*, and then I turn my back on the *Trevi*.

I toss the coin in a high arc over my left shoulder. As I hear the plonk of it breaking the water I smile in the knowledge that my return to Rome is now guaranteed. Based upon what I have shared with you, are you surprised that this is what I choose to believe?

The Son She Never Had

Luca inhaled deeply and then parked his cigarette in the ashtray. He turned to me wearing a very decisive expression and said:

"You know..." Luca paused, *"... you are the son she never had."*

"What do you mean?" I asked him pointedly.

"You know it, the good son, the one she had always hoped for...but the one she never actually had...until you finally arrived!" he replied and punctuated with his mischievous staccato laugh.

"Sei pazzo*!" I exclaimed, *"She has two sons, you and Simone."*

"Yes, I am...but not about this. Somehow you have become the third son; the good one that she now measures us against. The one she now uses against us!" he proclaimed as he reached for the coffee that his mother Elide had brought us only moments ago.

How did this happen? When did this happen? Luca's comments put me in a reflective mood and caused me to start leafing through a mental scrapbook of memories of my previous visits with *la famiglia*.

Our story together began in the *primavera* of 1989 when I arrived in

* See Glossary P.200

Rome for a three day visit. Immediately I was confronted with an interesting cultural difference. The planned duration of my three day visit was deemed to be unacceptably short. After all I was *famiglia* even though I had only just met them. Luca was the exception as we had been friends for a couple of years by then.

This was radically new thinking for me since I subscribed to the fish theory of travel. *"House guests are like fish in your refrigerator. Best to throw them out once three days have passed!"* A wise Dutch friend once told me that, and it has stayed with me over the decades.

Overcoming my cultural reluctance to be an imposition, I put an offer on the table I hoped would satisfy them. I would extend my visit to an entire week. Their facial expressions, eyebrows arched delicately to induce guilt, told me that this was not a serious offer.

My saving grace was that I had a commitment in France in eight days time. This was a tangible reason to leave, though barely justifiable in their eyes. After all, as the old saying goes all roads lead to Rome, so why would one need to go anywhere else?

It was 1992 before I returned to Rome and my adopted *famiglia*. *'What took you so long to come back?'* was initially in their eyes. This was quickly overshadowed by the epic welcome of their beaming smiles, warm embraces, and the traditional kiss on both cheeks.

Over the first glass of wine Ilio, the family patriarch, asked me about '*my igloo in Canada*' in his usual deadpan tone as the rest of *la famiglia* laughed. Let the games begin I thought, and deftly changed the subject by asking Sir Ilio why he no longer topped up my wine glass as he had during my previous visit.

His reply was very matter of fact:

"*Roberto, on your first visit you were a guest, and now you are famiglia. Well, famiglia serves themselves and you can reach the wine from where you sit...can't you?*"

Elide, his wife, smiled and rolled her eyes as if to say: '*Here we go again, just like old times.*' We share a special relationship Elide and I, and it was from this relationship that the '*son she never had*' myth grew. You see I don't speak much Italian and Elide does not speak any English. Our communication is an eclectic mixture of spoken word, hand gestures, facial expressions, and pantomime.

Luca, ever the curious one, began to analyze how his mother and I were able to communicate. Under cross-examination one evening, Luca queried his mother in Italian and then myself in English about our topics of discussion that afternoon. Our responses were eerily similar and Luca was pleasantly baffled at how two people who do not share a common language could still manage to communicate.

Eventually, after careful deliberation, he decided that it must be a case of reincarnation. Elide and I had been mother and son in a previous life he hypothesized. His theory, he proudly announced, neatly explained our ability to communicate with each other in the absence of a common language. He went on to support his argument with evidence of my affinity for Italy and my seamless adaptation to the lifestyle.

Luca was definitely on a roll now; and he concluded his case by coming full circle back to his starting point: I was the son that she had never had in this life, and the son that she had once had in a previous life. Elide smiled at this 'theory' and informed her son "Sei molto pazzo!".

Speculation and hypothesizing are beautiful pastimes in Italy. Old world cultural traditions weave the social fabric into a rich tapestry that serves to keep daily life entertaining.

Living in the 'new world' in a young country like Canada, I can't help but be fascinated by the old world pedigree of the Romans. Their storied heritage is an ever-present touchstone for their modern descendants. A sacred talisman that can end a debate at any point since any challenge to the pedigree can be causally dismissed as 'new world' thinking. Luca has enjoyed using this tactic against me on many occasions.

Notwithstanding their ties to their past, most Romans that I have met display an eager curiosity about the ways of the 'new world'. However, the caveat is that their interest rarely translates into an adoption of these 'new world' ways. Unsurprisingly, the roots of the old ways run too deep, as Luca has reminded me with statements like: *"Roberto, Romans have been doing it this way for over 2000 years. Who are we to question the enduring traditions born of such an Empire?"*

I experienced one of these *'traditions'* first hand a few years ago when I was recruited to help Luca pick up some appliances and kitchen cabinets for his new apartment. What I initially thought of as simply a chance to help my friend, and in a small way repay him for all the kindness that he and his family had shown me, became so much more. I was treated to a fantastic cultural experience that eventually led me to a paradigm shift.

Meeting up with Luca, his brother Simone, and their father Sir Ilio at the rendezvous point, I innocently inquired *"Where's the truck?"*

"What truck?" Simone asked.

"The truck that we will use to pick up and deliver the appliances, furniture and kitchen cabinets." I replied.

Simone gave me his shy smile while Luca burst out laughing. When he had recovered himself, Luca translated my words for Sir Ilio. In response he raised his eyebrows and nodding in my direction he exclaimed, *"This one needs help doesn't he?"* Sir Ilio then turned his gaze to me and punctuated his words with a disappointed shrug to indicate that he had expected better of me.

Luca and Simone both shared a laugh at my expense. Luca then patiently explained to me that my idea of renting a moving van was an extravagance. In Rome you simply call your father and brother, and / or an uncle or three who arrive on the appointed day with their vehicles.

Having my idea laughed at, and so quickly dismissed without even the slightest consideration put me on the defensive. I had fallen in their esteem, especially Sir Ilio's. I needed to reclaim that, or at the very least, to mitigate the damage. How could I manage to convince them of the merits of renting a truck today?

Well, that ship had already sailed and nothing I said was going to make it change its course. Pointing out to them the efficiencies of renting a truck were only grudgingly acknowledged. They were even more stubborn than I was. It was time to let this go and to get refocused on the task of helping my friends.

In the end, it took a few hours and some heated debate over a couple of espressos. The result was two fully loaded cars, one of which had a refrigerator tied to its roof rack and a dishwasher protruding from its open rear hatch. The other car had a kitchen table, turned upside down, strapped to its roof. Upon that table rested a stack of kitchen cabinets that was crowned with several chairs. This eclectic sculpture was painstakingly lashed together by Sir Ilio with a series of small ropes and cords. To my eyes it looked like a disaster waiting patiently to happen. No one else seemed concerned.

The dynamic of our mission had changed. I had been quiet for a while now, but in that moment I felt compelled to speak. Hoping to appeal to their sense of reason I expressed my concern over the safety and the legality of navigating these *'sculptures'* through rush hour traffic.

Sir Ilio shook his head slowly and asked his sons: *"What are we going to do with this one? He still hasn't clued in."*

"Don't worry Roberto, it will be fine." Luca said as he gave me a reassuring pat on the shoulder. I was not reassured in the least. I made one last ditch attempt to stave off the pending calamity.

"We still have time to rent a moving van?" I suggested hopefully.

"We don't rent moving vans! Andiamo!" the three of them barked at me in unison, and with that the matter was closed to any further discussion.

"Fine, suit yourselves." I muttered under my breath.

Predictably, the drive to the apartment was painstakingly slow. It was an extremely circuitous route that took our bizarre caravan down all manner of side streets and goat paths. We could have walked there faster, I thought to myself. With every corner and pothole I braced for the inevitable crash of tables, chairs, and cabinets as they escaped the car roof and briefly won their freedom; only to end up splintered in the street. In a perverse way, I almost hoped for this outcome so that I could tell them that I had told them so.

Thankfully, I never got that opportunity. We arrived at *via Turatti* with our cargo intact, and my *Nostradamus*-like disaster prophecies unfulfilled.

Sir Ilio began untying his collection of knots in order to liberate the furniture and cabinets. While Sir Ilio was occupied with that job, Simone and I tackled getting the dishwasher and the refrigerator up to the apartment. Luca enjoyed a cigarette as he surveyed the street life.

As our work wound down, it suddenly dawned on me what the lesson of the day was. I realized that a process could be inefficient and disorganized, and yet therein lay its simple truth. My *famiglia* had shown me that although the task of moving was what had brought us together, our true mission was to enjoy our time with each other as the task was being accomplished.

The memories of our day together were like a beautiful painting. What began as a blank canvas was now covered with laughter, debates, discovery, cooperation and accomplishment. Our 'painting' would have lacked depth, character and meaning if we had chosen to accomplish this move as quickly and efficiently as possible.

With the mission completed, our visit now shifted to the dinner table. Naturally, the events of the day were discussed as Elide was very curious to learn how they had unfolded. Sir Ilio, ever the diplomat, gave her a succinct version that did not make any mention of my preference for new world moving techniques.

However, Luca felt no shame in crowing about the triumph of old world over new world as he savored another cigarette. Clearly, diplomacy is a trait that Luca has not inherited from his father.

Elide enjoys his story but glares disapprovingly at the cigarette. As soon as it has been stubbed out in the ashtray, immediately the next one is lit. She scolds Luca with a *'Basta!'*, then turns to me and exclaims that he is *'Incorrigible!'* Refocusing her attention on Luca, she admonishes him for not being be more like me.

"Ah yes..." he replies, *"...the good son who doesn't smoke; the son you never had!"* punctuated with an exclamation point of laughter.

This response elicits a dismissive wave from Elide, who rises from the table and escapes from the expanding cloud of blue smoke by departing for the kitchen to begin the coffee.

The *tavola*, I quickly realized on my first visit to Italy, is the primary hub for social interactions. Whether it's lunch at a *trattoria* with friends or colleagues, or dinner at home with *famiglia*, spirited discussions at the table are the norm.

The topics are free range and run the gamut from the local events to world affairs. Politics and the state of the economy seem to be universal favorites. That is really no surprise given the copious amount of incendiary material provided by Berlusconi during his reign.

As a *stranieri*, my relationship with the *tavola* is a special one; well it is to me in any case. Hailing from a culture where food and family meals around the table hold less daily importance, experiencing the *tavola* in Italy was a revelation of sorts for me. It felt like I had finally arrived at the place that I had been searching for. The generous invitation to take a seat at the *tavola* told me that I was finally with my *famiglia*.

Reflecting back on it after all these years leads me to think that I probably ate my way into *la famiglia's* hearts. In all honesty this came quite naturally to me as I have a healthy appetite and a deep appreciation of Italian cuisine.

'*Complimenti, mi piace molto!*' is an important phrase that I learned early on, and have used often as Elide is an absolute genius in the kitchen. She never seems to get tired of hearing me say this. We are in harmony, as I expect to continue to enjoy her delicious cuisine and to pay her this compliment for many years to come.

And yet, I have always wanted to do something more than simply pay her compliments. For years I have suggested that we open a small *trattoria*, and each time I do, the response is the same. Elide's smile says she is flattered, and she tells me that it is a nice idea, simply to humour me I suspect. Yet her eyes betray her as they dismiss my suggestion as *'new world'* thinking.

Typically, the conversation goes something like this: I muse aloud that a *trattoria* is a lot of work, and deftly switch gears into my next idea: a book of signora Elide's recipes. *"La Cucina di Elide. It's a natural!"* I proclaim.

With the hope of enlisting an ally, I attempt to draw Luca into the conversation by playing the guilt card:

"Since you have no sister, when your Mama leaves this earth so do her recipes. Unless we take action now!" I say to him.

"Senti, Roberto..." he reluctantly agrees *"Of course on the one hand you are correct. However, once again you are complicating my life with yet another one of your seemingly endless supply of projects."* And then he sighs, shrugs his shoulders and reaches for his cigarettes.

Elide scowls at him, emits a plaintiff *'Basta!'*, then shakes her head in resignation and retreats from the smoke yet again. In the sanctuary of her kitchen, she starts a second round of coffees for her sons. The one she has always had and the one that she has never had.

Dinner with Ciro

Delicious aromas wafting from a nearby window are seducing my nose. Stepping closer, I peer through that window and catch a glimpse of some *Nonas** toiling over an array of bubbling pots atop the stoves. My stomach grumbles insistently in response to these sights and smells. I need to reset my focus, and so I turn my attention back to the street and scan the small crowd clustered outside the *trattoria*. The reset does not last, and I turn to Anna and Antonio with my plea.

" I'm sooooo hungry! Can't we find another place to eat? This can't possibly be worth the wait!"

These comments are born of a visceral hunger that compels me to toss them out in frustration to my companions.

Their faces broaden into smiles as they exchange knowing glances. Anna, taking hold of my arm as if to anchor me to that very spot, exclaimed:

"Senti, Roberto it'll be worth the wait. Trust me."

I turn to Antonio for support but he only nods in agreement with her. That is the second battle I have lost today to these two. The first was an hour or so ago when the discussion on where to dine was opened. Predictably, I cast my vote for the *Antica Osteria del Gallo*, my

See Glossary P. 201

favorite pizzeria in *Napoli*.

Everyone agreed that it was an excellent choice. However, there was also a small problem for Anna and Antonio. The *Osteria* was on the other side of town, sandwiched between the *Fontanelle* and *Sanita* neighbourhoods, near the foot of *Martedi* hill. It was not a drive that either of them was eager to make in rush hour traffic.

The chance to visit with our friend Rosario, the owner and *pizzaiolo* of the *Osteria*, did not convince them. Nor did visions of the cozy warmth of the brazier, full of glowing embers from the pizza oven, that would be placed beneath our table to ward of the November chill. I even tried to appeal to their sense of tradition and *famiglia* by reminding them that the *Osteria* had been owned and operated by the same family since 1898. Their unified response to my plea was immediate and non-negotiable: we would go there next week...for lunch...when the traffic was manageable.

Just then, a round man in a white t-shirt and wire rimmed John Lennon glasses burst through the door and barked: *"Capello nero per due"*. Two people emerged from the crowd, one wearing a black hat of course, and proceeded into the restaurant grinning as if they had just won the lottery. My stomach protested, partly in hunger, mostly in envy.

"That's Ciro, the owner."

Anna informed me, as he scurried back inside the *trattoria*.

Seeking to distract me from the wait and my hunger, Antonio asked me about my recent *passeggiata*.

"Have you ever seen the Potato Man?"

I asked him. He shook his head no in response.

"I chanced upon him this afternoon in the Quartieri Spagnoli. He was engaged in commerce at its most basic level. As I was walking, I was startled by a shout from above. I looked up to see a woman lowering a red plastic bucket on a string down from her fifth floor balcony towards a man on the street."

I paused, hoping to add some suspense to a story that was in desperate need of it.

"When the man turned to grab the bucket, I saw that he had a 5kg bag of potatoes tucked under his other arm. Potato Man put four spuds in the bucket and it was hauled back up to the balcony. Deemed to be acceptable, after passing inspection, the spuds were removed and the bucket was lowered again. This time its cargo was a few coins to settle the bill. Paid in full, Potato Man resumed his shuffle down the cobbled streets in search of his next client."

Thankfully, Anna rescued me from having to continue my story. *"Roberto, look!"* She directed my attention to a noisy *Vespa* scooter that was straining under its load of a family of five.

The smallest child spilled over from the handlebar basket, limbs and upper torso dangling over its rim with the driver, his father, right behind him. Next up was the middle child, sandwiched between his mother and father. The eldest was perched on the last few centimeters of the saddle and clinging to his mother seated just in front. Their radiant smiles were testament to their enjoyment of this transit adventure. The ride home in a few hours would be a similar adventure; of this I had no doubt.

Enter stage right! Ciro emerged to record the new arrivals. *"Vespa gialla"* he announced while scribbling on his pad. Brow furrowed and lips twisted into a grimace of intense concentration, he barked: *"Moto Man!"*, while simultaneously crossing off his list with a dramatic flourish.

"That's us. Veni!" Anna and Antonio exclaimed as they excitedly pushed me towards the door. Moto Man was the nickname our trio was tagged with, owing to the vintage black leather biker jacket Antonio happened to be wearing.

Shortly after taking our seats, it dawned on me that this was not your typical *trattoria*. The wait outside offered no hint of the carnival-like atmosphere inside. Ciro's circus is a raucous, no frills affair. The waiters whirl like dervishes, between the tables of animated diners, as they balance trays loaded with food and drink above their heads.

A few photocopied menus circulate from table to table as the diners huddle together over their cherished copy. Deciphering the faded hieroglyphics elicits much laughter and debate about what to order.

My first reaction was '*Is this a joke? How can a restaurant not have a printed menu for every diner?*' Soon my table was sharing a menu, and a moment. This nearly illegible sheet of paper was bringing us together as we discussed its various options. I was beginning to feel like I was in a Fellini movie!

"*Oh, we have luck tonight!*" Anna announced. "*pasta e fagioli is on the menu. You must try it!*" I have every intention of following her advice but of course as the old saying goes: *man plans, God laughs.* Unfortunately, this dish is so popular they have already run out of it, our waiter explains. He seems genuinely empathetic to our disappointment and offers recommendations of other tempting dishes.

"*Creeeeash*" goes the aluminum baking tray that was purposely thrown to the floor. Everyone in the restaurant stops eating and turns to see the source of the commotion. It's Ciro, grinning impishly as he stoops to pick up the tray and chides the patrons for watching him while their delicious meals are getting cold.

The diners laugh, "*Oh that Ciro!*" someone exclaims. "*Oh that Ciro!*" Ciro retorts mockingly. The waiters smile knowingly, and Ciro races back outside to check the queue.

Minutes later, a table in the corner is so engrossed in their meal and each other that they fail to notice Ciro edging stealthily towards them. Their attention becomes riveted on him after he slams a large metal cooking spoon down on the edge of their table and then innocently inquires, *"Are you enjoying your meal?"*

Before they have a chance to respond, Ciro spins away to land at an adjacent table. He loudly berates these regulars for eating too slowly, for not ordering enough, and for taking up too much space. The table under attack responds to this staged scolding with an eruption of laughter, which quickly spreads throughout the *trattoria*.

The spotlight is stolen from Ciro by a waiter who appears with a basket of oranges and a bunch of bananas raised aloft as he clownishly asks, *"Who wants desert?"* This elicits renewed eruptions of laughter. Words simply do not do this moment justice. It falls into the *'you had to be there...'* category.

Ciro quickly reclaims the spotlight by asking a nearby waiter to open a window. When the waiter asks why, Ciro points at the table of regulars and replies, *"These ones are done eating so throw them out the window and into the street, then get the table ready for the next group."* Ciro then bolts outside, yet again, to assess the waiting crowd.

Just when I thought this place could not get any wilder the cashier gets in on the act. A client settling their tab proffers a tip which the cashier makes an exaggerated point of dropping into the communal tip can while yelling, *"Another one for us boys!"* The waiters roar their approval in unison. This drama is repeated many more times over the course of the evening. The diners clearly appreciate both the service and the show provided by Ciro and his boys.

We have finished our meal and have agreed to take *una passeggiata.* As we are deciding between *Gelateria Scimia* or *Café Gambrinus,* our waiter arrives with our bill and much to our surprise a piping hot bowl of freshly made *pasta e fagioli.*

We are absolutely stuffed, and so politely tell him that we did not order this dish. He just smiles and gives the bowl a gentle nudge further onto our table to tempt us. We clutch at our bellies and plead with him that none of us can possibly manage another bite. Dismissing our pleas, he advises us that we will regret it if we do not try it; and besides, it's on the house.

Unable to face the possibility of offending him by refusing his generosity, we are left with only one course of action; returning our napkins from the table to our laps. With weary sighs we pick up our spoons to resume eating.

Predictably, the allocation of this dish is anything but fair with me being given half of it, and my two friends each taking responsibility for a mere quarter share of it. When I protest this injustice, they quickly remind me that I am the guest so I deserve the bigger share because I will never get another chance to try it.

I remind them that I am in *Napoli* for another five weeks and will certainly return to enjoy another meal at Ciro's. They counter that the menu changes every day, and so *pasta e fagioli* likely won't be on offer on my next visit.

History is repeating itself yet again as I am making no headway whatsoever in debate with these two. I resign myself to attempting to clear my bowl. I have a better chance of accomplishing this than of winning the debate. Pausing between spoonfuls, I see our waiter poised by the cashier and intently watching the outcome. I am successful by the narrowest of margins. Our waiter is pleased; a *'See, I knew you would love it!'* expression adorning his face.

When we arrive at the cashier to settle our bill, it becomes our moment in the spotlight. As our tip is accepted and announced, we receive a roar of appreciation from the waiters.

As we step out of the *trattoria* and back onto the cobblestones to commence our *passeggiata,* I muse aloud about what a unique experience that was.

"How so?" Antonio asked.

"Are you kidding? Ciro and the waiters are certainly unique! Oh, and I have never walked out of a restaurant being cheered by the staff before. That is pretty unusual." I answer.

"*This is Napoli Roberto. Here we expect the unexpected, and we have a deep appreciation for it!*" replied Antonio.

"*Yes, it is truly as Antonio says, and especially when you have dinner with Ciro!*" Anna chimed in.

Someone Always Leaves – IV

Honestly, it does not happen very often to me. I can probably count the number of times on one hand; which is precisely why those few exceptions really stand out in my mind.

At first glance, she left me more breathless. Italian women are the natural embodiment of style and beauty in my opinion. I felt a strong intuitive flash that there was something much deeper and more complex about her. Something well beyond, and yet complimentary, to her physical beauty. Time proved my intuition to be correct.

We were introduced at a business function. Our short conversation left me captivated and wondering how I could see her again. I reached out to her but she was not ready, and so I stopped reaching. A few months later, fate intervened and we ended up working in the same office. Unfortunately, she was already involved romantically with the business owner who had given her the job and was assisting her with her immigration.

The chemistry between us was palpable. Yet, there was also much uncertainty. Interacting with each other day in and day out eventually became a perilous situation for both of us. My career and her relationship were at risk. It was those risks, as well our earlier missed opportunities, that precluded us from being open to the possibility of exploring this attraction further.

Humour became our mutual outlet. It was a way for us to enjoy our chemistry within the confines of the polite formality of the office. Our humour was spontaneous and often it cast us in the roles of mock adversaries. Looking back on it now, I don't think we were fooling anyone in the office, except maybe ourselves.

One day she ambushed me with an exaggerated sweetness. Jokingly suggesting that I should marry her immediately so that she could stay in Canada forever. If only she had known how much I would have liked to explore that idea with her. Instead, because there were colleagues around, I laughed at her pseudo-proposal and played along, asking her to tell me more about her grand plan.

She smiled and continued by explaining to me that she already had her ring picked out, and so all I had to do was accompany her to *Cartier* and buy it. Then I would put it on her finger in front of a few hundred people one Saturday afternoon this September, and that would be that. Pretty simple really, she exclaimed with a most seductive expression.

Playing to the audience, I asked her if she knew about Canadian engagement traditions. She admitted that she was unfamiliar with them. I explained to her that in Canada the custom was for the bride-to-be to buy a Harley-Davidson motorcycle for her fiancé; then and only then could he purchase the ring for her.

I had her half-convinced until the snickering of our colleagues tipped her off. With mock seriousness she asked me when I would like to go motorcycle shopping. I told her that I would get back to her after I checked my schedule for an opening.

"Tanto piu ti amo quanto piu mi fuggi, o bello!" She answered me as she drew very close, wrapped her arm around mine, and asked me if I had understood. I told her that I did not understand her words but that I really liked how they had sounded.

In response, she cupped her hand gently to my ear and whispered: *"They are Baudelaire's words: The more I love you the more you flee from me, my darling."* With that she stepped away, paused to give me a wicked grin, and then departed for her office. Checkmate, very well played.

Our joking abruptly stopped a few weeks later when she decided to return to Italy for a job opportunity. It turned out to be more than that, as she confessed to me later. On her last day in the office she casually asked for my email so that we might stay in contact. I gave it to her thinking all the while that at best there would be a few emails talking about the weather and similar trivial minutiae.

As it turned out, I could not have been more wrong. Once we became separated by the ocean, our feelings for each other quickly emerged. The emails were daily, and the phone calls lasted for hours. Occasionally we even surprised each other with hand-written letters sent via old-fashioned mail.

Our bond grew as we confessed memories of our impressions of and attractions to each other during the brief time that we had shared in the office. These confessions inevitably led to questions:

Why didn't you say anything?

Well why didn't you?

How come you never invited me for a coffee?

I wanted to, believe me.

Oh, if only you had we would be together now!

We had been so tantalizingly close. Despite those moments of physical proximity, we had been unable to truly find each other, or to face what had been right in front of us. It was the safety of the distance between us now that gave us the opportunity, and perhaps the courage, to open up and really begin to discover each other; finally.

As the months passed, we became very close. Well as close as phone calls, emails, and letters will permit. One day she told me that she was my *Dolcezza**. That word captivated me. It was delicious, exotic, and so very seductive compared to its English equivalent: sweetheart.

She sent me photos of herself exploring her hometown. The one I

*See Glossary P.202

recall vividly was of her on the beach. She had just emerged from the ocean. Her hair was slicked back and beads of water glistened all over her bronzed face and torso. Her smile and eyes radiated pure happiness. She was beautiful. She was my *Dolcezza*. A few weeks later, I sent her photos back to her. Shortly afterwards, I found myself wishing that I had not.

Unsurprisingly, we soon needed more than emails and phone calls. She made the decision to return to Canada to pursue a Master's Degree and to be with me. Planning for her return created an exciting new reality for us to contemplate. We were finally going to be together in body, as well as mind and spirit. This new reality gave rise to new feelings, a new urgency, and thus a new tone to our interactions. A heightened sense of anticipation took hold as we imagined of our future together. Everything seemed possible now.

Then, just before her return to Canada, it all came crashing down. Fate often enjoys reminding us that what we ran away from in a hurry yesterday is what will catch up to us tomorrow, or the next day. She had left some unfinished business behind when she had returned to Italy the previous summer. She had never really ended things with the business owner; at least not with the proper degree of finality that had been required. It was more complicated than that of course. Isn't it always?

Staying silent about her return to Canada was not an option. Yet the path to opening this conversation eluded her. Our story was beginning to mirror the tragic comedy of a *Puccini* opera.

When she finally did open the conversation with the business owner it did not go very well. Later, when we spoke, she spared me the unpleasant details and focused on communicating the rationale behind her decision to me. She had changed. In her mind she could no longer be my *Dolcezza*.

And so, she left...Us.

Predictably, I was devastated. I could not reconcile what I was now hearing with what I had just recently heard. We had been planning our life together. Now she was telling me that she would be returning to Canada to complete her studies, and that she needed her space without any distractions. I had lost her.

I could not understand how we had ended up here; now so far away from our dreams after we had almost realized them. The choice that she had made brought her closer to some of her dreams, at the expense of our dreams. In her place, I might have made the same choice. This choice, perhaps the best one available to her in that moment, was what would ultimately cost us our chance to be together. The dominoes had begun falling.

Through gritted teeth, I voiced my disbelief. I had trouble finding my thoughts and the words to express them. I am not telling the truth. I did have the words, but I kept them to myself because they were angry and hurtful words, and so they were of no use to us in that moment.

On a sub-conscious level, I knew that neither of us deserved that anger. It would only have further opened the wounds of our mutual disappointment; and they were already deep enough. Things could change. I wanted so desperately to believe that.

Words quickly failed us both, and so we retreated into the silence of our thoughts. This was unnatural, and so very different from the phone calls that we had enjoyed so much in the past. But this was now, and in our silence a heavy sadness took root. Why is it that important things are so difficult to say; whereas meaningless things are so easily expressed?

Was she wishing for me to give her the words she needed to convince her to welcome me back into her life? Only she could have answered that question. In that precise moment, I had persuaded myself that nothing I could have said would have changed the outcome. Her newly chosen path was both defined and decided. Neither of us had had the courage to speak about what remained unspoken. Our final call ended with a polite goodbye.

My heart was engulfed in a black abyss of disappointment and hurt. Where there had been calls, emails, letters filled with hope, plans and magic, there was now darkness where the fragments of our shattered dreams resided.

Fortunately, it was only a few weeks later when I was liberated from the abyss. My freedom arrived in the form of a most unexpected surprise. Someone resurfaced whom I had thought had been lost forever. Her name was *Elle* and we had shared something very special at one time. As it turned out, it was welcoming *Elle* back into my life that led me to make a tragic error in judgment. Patience, we will get to that soon enough.

Unsurprisingly, *Dolcezza* and I had forsaken all contact. Surprisingly, she reached out to me one day, after months of silence. It turned out that she had returned to Toronto, and had moved ahead with some of her dreams as planned. She was all settled in now, and wanted to see me. It had been just over a year since we had been in the same room together. I felt compelled to see her after what we had shared, as well as what we had almost shared.

We met at her apartment downtown, near the University. When she opened the door she was even more beautiful than I had remembered. She was wearing a light grey sweater and jeans. Her brown eyes sparkled with life. Her smile was captivating in its warmth. Her tan was a sensual dark bronze. She was absolutely stunning! Her beauty left me *e respiro immaginifico*; just as it had the very first time that I had seen her. Yet, it was different from that first time. I now knew of her inner beauty as she had bared her soul to me, and allowed me to know her in a most rare and intimate way.

Initially, she seemed a bit nervous. It was unusually cute and endearing because I knew it would quickly vanish, and that I would never see her in this way again.

We started talking, and soon we were laughing. It felt really good, almost like old times...almost. She intuitively sensed something was different. She asked me if it was *Elle*; the woman I was with before I had met her. I confirmed that it was. *"Then there is no chance?"* she asked me. It seemed to me as if she had already decided that she knew my answer. There is always a chance. However, in that moment I was blind to it because of the choices that *Dolcezza* and I had recently made.

And so I left...Us.

Well, that is not truly accurate. At that point in time there was no Us. Perhaps what I walked away from on that day was an opportunity. Had *Dolcezza* been looking to begin our story again?

In that moment, in her apartment, there was no doubt in my mind. I was truly happy with *Elle*, and so re-starting our story was not in the realm of possibility for me. A little over a year later, *Elle* was gone and *Dolcezza* had returned to Italy, again. Destiny never seemed to favour our being together.

Many years later, and quite by accident, I finally stumbled upon the truth. This came about due to a surprising convergence of events which awakened some long-forgotten memories for me. That awakening gave rise to the desire to seek out a very specific moment from my past. There are no accidents, a friend of mine is too fond of reminding me.

It was our email correspondence that revealed this truth to me. In those pages *Dolcezza* and I had opened our souls to each other. I do not have the words to describe the rare beauty of this to you. Reading them again was an epiphany! I felt immense joy over what we had shared. Yet, this joy was partially overshadowed by a profound sadness that we had lost this. As I write these words, it feels as raw to me as if it had been yesterday.

The truth of this moment struck me like a bolt of lightning, giving me the uncomfortable sensation that I was in a free-fall. Finally, after all this time had passed, I could see the truth. When I walked out of her apartment on that day so many years ago I had missed it completely. How did I not see that I had just walked away from the woman whom I should have spent my life with?

When truths are discovered, inevitably questions arise. I can't help but wonder what our journey together might have been if we had of made different choices. Two choices in particular stand apart from the rest. One choice for each of us as it turned out. I can tell you that I have accumulated very few regrets over the course of my life. Walking out of her apartment that day is now one of them; le *grand amour perdu*.

Over the years, I have passed through her town a few of times. Always on my way to somewhere else. I know that *Dolcezza* is no longer there; at least I am pretty sure that she is not. Last I heard she was in Milan, but that was decades ago.

Passing by that beach town where she grew up always causes me to wonder about her. You can never step in the same river twice; no matter what your memories of the past are whispering to you. Perhaps, the next time that I pass by, I will get off the train to have a look around. I promise.

Unusual Storms

It is very early, and I am enjoying the silence. It is approaching the time when night punches the clock and hands over the keys to a new day. I am sitting in the middle of a street, and hugging my knees tightly to my chest so as to make myself as small as possible.

The street seems both familiar and unfamiliar to me. I think I am still in Milan, but that is just a gut feeling at this point. If certainty is a continuum, then I currently find myself at the almost-certain-but-not-positively-certain end of it. These are strange days, indeed.

Abstract images in a multitude of colours, dancing reflections in the pooled water, have made the street come alive. This spontaneous art show originates from the lighted signage on the buildings lining each side of the street. I prefer the neon ones. I always have.

In my left hand I hold an umbrella to shield me from the downpour. The umbrella is black and of compact size. In this moment, I long for a much larger umbrella as the protection offered by this one is barely adequate. It is an old umbrella that has served me very well on my travels. Inevitably, I wonder for how many more storms it will be able to offer me protection.

My concern is a valid one as this is an unusual storm. In addition to the normal precipitation, there is a deluge of beeps, buzzes, dings, bells, whistles and other assorted e-noises. It is raining cell phones you see. As they drop from the sky, they bombard me with emails, phone calls, *WhatsApp*, *Messenger*, *Instagram*, and texts. This uncontrolled fire hose of information, questions, requests, demands, notifications, reminders and calls to action are an incessant assault on my attention.

Many of the phones have bounced off my umbrella and into the puddles in the street. Once there, they briefly produce a blaze of sparks and flashes, before they go dark and turn silent for eternity. I enjoyed this. The phones that avoided landing in the puddles soon meet a similar fate as the accumulation of rain seeping into their innards eventually takes its toll.

The storm has passed. I get up to stretch and then collapse my umbrella. The street is unsurprisingly empty at this hour. I begin walking east, away from the *Duomo**. Clearly, I have now moved along the continuum to reach absolute certainty. I am in Milan.

Before the storm, I had been up on the roof of the *Duomo* enjoying the panoramic view of Milan. I was up there taking photos of the ornate roof with its many statues and decorative stonework.

I feel something gently strike me. This continues with increasing frequency. I stop walking and look up to see that miniature people are dropping from the sky now. I quickly re-open the umbrella and raise it up to cover myself again. Sitting down in the street seems like the best option, so that is what I do.

*See Glossary p.202

How can I best describe these miniature people to you? Well first of all, they are only slightly smaller in size than my left thumb. What is most striking about these *Minis* is that I know each of them. As I look over the various groups I instantly recognize family, friends, colleagues, girlfriends, and a variety of passing acquaintances.

Also, there are others who have briefly visited me on the periphery of my life. There are people that I met on trains and on planes. There are also people who have been spontaneously kind to me that I have never had the chance to re-pay, and vice versa.

Do you keep a reciprocity ledger? Don't you believe that it all evens out over time; and so keeping score is unnecessary? Anyhow, the common thread here is that I have directly interacted with each of these people, their full size versions, at some point in time.

As I gazed at the groups an interesting observation struck me. After they land, they seem to instinctively find their way to the niche group that they belong in. How do they know to do this? What does it all mean? These unanswerable questions have begun to pile up. I feel compelled to find their meanings. Instinctively, I know that it is an exercise in futility.

None of the miniatures speak. Some stand, while others sit. They all look directly at me. Many of them seem to wear expressions of anticipation. A few of them exhibit an air of friendliness in their smiles and in their eyes. Their silence is somewhat disconcerting to me. Should I break the silence and speak to them? Not just yet. I need to be patient and to give this more time, and more thought.

While I am thinking, I notice that a new group has formed: people who I saw once and then later wished that I had talked to. For the life of me I do not have a clue what their appearance means. Lost opportunities come to mind. Symbolic apparitions meant to prod me in a specific direction? To show me that in those moments I missed out on everything, as well as nothing at all.

I finally decide to address them, these groups of *Minis*. There is no response, other than their continued silence. A moment later, one of them steps forward. He is an Old Man, elegantly dressed in a dark navy blue suit, and sporting a wiry silver grey mustache. His eyes are piercingly blue. He clears his throat and begins to speak to me in French.

"The world is a better place because you and I each draw breath at the same time. Yesterday was the end of the beginning. Today is the beginning of the end. I will tell you the truth; but I will tell it to you in my own way, and only when the moment is ripe. You will need to trust my words, yet retain a degree of skepticism at the same time. Do you agree?"

I nodded in reply, and the Old Man proceeded:

"You seek to become more than you are. I hold that invitation open to you. The first step on your journey is to determine exactly when you became trapped in the mythology that you created? From there, with further reflection, in time you will discover the answer: kill your pride. It is the only way to reach the exit

from your maze."

I start to reply, but he cut me off and continued:

"Your mistake is a common one. It is the inability to gauge your location on the continuum of time. That leads you to hold onto a dream for much longer than you should. Believing that you still have all the time in the world, you stubbornly cling to your old ways that have occasionally brought you some small measure of success. The inescapable truth: you are running out of time. Now is the moment to wake-up to the reality that your delusions can only lead you to the empty place."

He paused to clear his throat again, then gave me a final serious look and said:

"Always remember that fortune favours the bold. Never forget that boldness has to be measured and prudent, not reckless and impudent. Timing and decisiveness are everything. Sometimes the Universe provides you with clues, a sign of the direction you are meant to take. Other times there is nothing, and you are left to act based on your best guess in that moment."

I do not have any response for him. I sense that he has more to say, and so I wait for him to continue. However, he does not continue, and instead he steps back into the group from which he had emerged.

Suddenly, I am overcome by a massive wave of fatigue. His words, and the very thought of the deep contemplation that they will require, have exhausted me. I stretch out on a nearby bench and fall into a heavy sleep. My umbrella lies beside me, awake and vigilant.

Interlude: Dreams in a White Room

From the simplest and purest of beginnings, the most complex situations frequently arise. Navigating through that complexity often leads full-circle back to the simplest of outcomes.

Three people find themselves in a white room. It is a completely white room: the walls, the marble flooring, the ceiling, the millwork, the furniture and the curtains are all brilliant white.

These three people are together, but they are not together. Two of them are sitting at a small bistro table that is positioned by a large window with the curtains pulled back. She is wearing an elegant white summer dress, while Her look is white linen pants and a white cotton shirt with no pockets. A rich sensual contrast is established by the deep bronze of their exposed skin against their bright white clothing.

The third person is a Man, and he is standing by another large window on the other side of the room, and away from them. The Man is wearing a black suit; it is the only non-white object in the room.

An infinite number of scenarios are possible in the white room. However, there is only one possible outcome. The notion that the result this specific time could be any different is absurd. The outcome is always the same, and it will always be the same, to a greater or a lesser degree. It is those familiar feelings of being incrementally emptier at the end of it, as well as a depletion of what remains to be given to the next occurrence. Those feelings will travel home with at least one of the three after they leave the white room.

"What are you thinking about now?" was Her question.

"I don't know..." She replied.

"You HAVE to know!" was Her emphatic response.

That which initially attracted, suddenly is repellent. Where it gets surreal is when something exists between two worlds; paralyzed in a limbo of indecision. No longer attractive, but not yet repellent either. It is that broken toaster that sits up on a shelf in the garage waiting to be fixed. It will never be fixed, and yet there is a distinct inability to let go of it once and for all.

"This is not about me. I am peripheral, external to you. I wish that you could feel how liberating that is. Even if only for the briefest of moments, to catch a glimpse of the existence of a better way. The recognition that the life which you claim to desire is within your grasp, if only you could get out of your own way. Only you can decide to leave the empty space. It really has nothing whatsoever to do with me."

She offered, and then went on to tell Her:

"In the beginning, there were so many things that I wanted to experience with you. Eventually I realized that majority of them were never going to

happen. That realization arrived with the passage of time as I began to see that you were hollowed out and consumed by the accumulation of your fears."

Their shadows grew longer on the floor as the light shifted incrementally in relation to the tall slender windows of the vintage apartment. The silence was uncomfortable, yet necessary. Without asking, She poured a glass of water for each of them.

The Man continued to gaze out the window. He was not listening to them. He was lost in thought about the colour of fear. Is it Black? A murky world of darkness where the unseen unfolds obscured by shadows? Is it White? A world of such brightness that we are unable to look directly at it, where the unseen remains hidden in plain sight? In both of these worlds, the Black and the White, our minds are compelled to fill in the void left by the unseen. Often, our imaginations spawn visions far more disturbing than actual reality could ever be.

There was a tense silence in the white room. Finally, the stalemate was broken by Her.

"Now what are you thinking about? Are you thinking about me?" was Her re-opening.

A smile cracked, and then She replied:

"Sure, about you and about Us, every so often. True confessions: The most recent time that I did, the memories were unpleasant. I recalled how tired I became watching you struggle with yourself. On occasion, when your need was

more than you could handle, you reached out to me. I gave of myself to you then, freely and with compassion. Afterwards, you admitted to me that in those few moments I had helped you to feel better about life. I wondered how you are able to live in that perpetual cycle. There has to be more to life than that. It cannot always be just about you. I am sorry; I know that is a little harsh."

Her immediate response was to sip Her water, in order to buy some time to consider those words. After repositioning Her glass on the table, Her words were offered:

"Remember that place that I showed you on one of our last walks? We were happy there. The photos that you took of us prove it. Photographs do a much better job of holding onto happiness than we ever can. It is the spaces in-between the happiness that are problematic for us. Those are the spaces where we always got stuck."

"Nice words, but they really don't change anything." She replied.

Her response was immediate and accusatory:

"Oh, but they change everything! They change the entire narrative...if you can open yourself to that. A new narrative could be our way forward, together. Why are you so dismissive of that?"

Very soon now, two of the three will have to join the others. It is something that they want to do, and it is also something that they have to do. However, some form of explanation for the others will be necessary. It is the very least that they can do.

It was discussed sporadically, tossed about as variations on a theme. What they might say about it, and to whom. To date they have not achieved any form of consensus on it. Thus the obvious choice, at this point, is to not say anything.

What the others will concoct in their imaginations will likely be far more colourful than the actual truth. Why not let them do all the work? In the absence of actual facts, they can only arrive at the flawed conclusions that their minds lead them to. None of this matters in any case, since no one believes the truth these days. These are the thoughts that occupy the Man as he gazes out the window.

"The idea of a new narrative is the product of a conversation that you had with yourself. It is precisely those types of conversations that are leading you to your emptiness. It is quite clear that this is very hard for you. I get that. You did not have to speak those actual words. What remains unspoken often reveals the most; particularly where you are concerned. It took me some time to figure that out."

She responded wearily, and then added:

"I will admit to being very surprised that you reached out to me this time. While not totally unexpected, it was still absolutely unexpected in this particular moment. Of course, you knew that my beliefs would oblige me to respond to you. In reality, it was a test in which you had little if anything to gain, while I had everything to lose. I passed it, and I feel that you should know that."

Without waiting for a reply, She got up and went around the table to Her side. Bending forward slightly, She tenderly kissed Her on both cheeks and then moved to Her ear, where She lingered just long enough to whisper:

"I am with Him now; and nothing is going to change that."

Those were the last words that She ever spoke to Her.

From the table, She went to the Man at the window. Taking his hand She said:

"We can leave now."

"Ready when you are." was my reply.

I awoke quite startled from that dream.

Looking down, I see the groups of *Minis* patiently staring up at me. The two women from the white room are there, in miniature now and in their own little group of two.

I sit up and gaze at the Pirelli tower, and then *Milano Centrale* behind me. I feel a strong urge to hop on a train now. What would that solve? Before I can answer myself, one of the *Minis* steps forward to address me. It is Pietro, the quirky chef of a *trattoria* that I frequent.

"The inherent paradox of the Road: it is too good to leave, yet it is not good enough to stay. As you know from experience, the freedom of the Road always

has a price. That price is agreed upon at the outset, and so it should be no surprise when the bill comes due. It is unavoidable, and so you must make your peace with it. Understand that by that point, you no longer have a choice in the matter. The deal is done and the plan is set in motion. You should never succumb to having regrets over your choices. It will only weaken your resolve."

Pietro smiled to signal that he was done, then he bowed and stepped back to rejoin his group. A response from me was not required, and so I also stepped back...and into my thoughts.

His words made me nostalgic and led me to contemplate the Road. My choices have brought me to the Road on several occasions over the years. Had I made other choices, meeting the Road might have been impossible, or at best markedly different than how it has unfolded. At the end of the day, it is the Universe that decides...everything! Still, as most people do, I enjoy deluding myself with the belief that my choices carry more influence than they actually do.

I begin to walk towards *Milano Centrale,* not to board a train, but in search of a coffee. The *Minis* do not follow me, and in fact they have dispersed in various directions opposite to the one I have taken.

Some truths are brutal in their clarity, while others make no sense whatsoever in the moment. For me, the *Minis* fall into the latter category, as the deeper meaning of their visit escapes me at this juncture in time. I briefly drift back to the words that the Old Man and Pietro offered me. I conclude that my visit with the *Minis* was a pleasant experience.

In the *Centrale*, a coffee bar was open. An oasis for bleary eyed travelers seeking the antidote for lack of sleep. The *barista* was sporting a *Betty Page*-meets-*Minnie Mouse* look, juxtaposed against a pair of naughty librarian glasses. Her style struck me as being pretty *avant-garde*, even for Milan. As she prepared the *cappuccino*, I wondered what it was about: individuality, rebellion, exuberance, fantasy or something else completely. Should I ask her?

Before I could decide, my mind was interrupted. I realized that the *barista* had not been among the groups of *Minis* who had visited with me earlier. This meant that a defining characteristic of the *Minis* was that they were all from my past. I made a mental note to look for this *barista* should I ever have the occasion to visit with the *Minis* again.

My coffee was ready. I collected it and moved to a stand – up table by a window overlooking the concourse. It was still very early and so the *Centrale* was not the chaotic hive of activity it normally is in the peak of the day. Out by the platforms even the trains looked sleepy to me, especially the older *Regionales* who had provided well over half a century of service by now.

As I sipped my coffee, my thoughts drifted away from the visuals of the concourse, and inexplicably arrived at memories of that time in the desert. It was only a few years ago that the wind sang us her song as the miles passed by. In the afternoons, we had the windows rolled down, old school. Just like back in the day...when there was no air-conditioning in vehicles. Those were simpler times; they were better times.

Out in the desert there is a lot of nothing, and we saw most of it. To my eyes, those desert towns consistently looked like the last stop on the long road to no more chances. The air hangs heavy with a tired desolation in those forgotten outposts.

An exit vision: as we pass a trailer park on the outskirts of town, I see a rotund fifty-something woman perched on her front porch. She has an iPhone in a sparkly gold case and a lit cigarette balanced in one hand, in her other hand is a lipstick stained cup of coffee...her morning ritual. She would definitely not be leaving that trailer park for a better life today. What has been seen cannot be unseen.

Without warning I abruptly leave the desert and return to the *Centrale*. My coffee is finished, so I get up to join life on the concourse. As I make my way to the main entry, I wonder where the *Minis* are at in this moment.

Upon exiting the *Centrale*, I feel moisture striking me. It is raining again. I reach for my umbrella, only to find that it is not with me. The umbrella is asleep on the bench, exactly where I left it over an hour ago.

That small event determines my fate. Doesn't it often happen in precisely this way? I turn around and re-enter the *Centrale*. Up on the *Partenze* board I note a train bound for *Ventimiglia* will be departing in seven minutes on *Binario* 3. I hustle back to the coffee bar and order a *cappuccino* and two *brioches* to go. With two minutes to spare, I am comfortably in my seat on that *Regionale*.

As the train slowly rolled out of the station, a thought crossed my mind: about midway through its journey this *Regionale* will make a stop in her town.

Years ago, in another life, I promised myself to disembark in that town and look for her if I ever had the chance. Today, that is no longer a promise, but merely a seductive memory from another time. Some bridges are never meant to be crossed. Some trains are meant to be ridden right to the last stop.

Someone Always Leaves - Coda

I had not been to the place in a long time; Pietro's place that is. It is rare that I manage to get to that part of the city these days. Of course, that is only a partially justifiable excuse. As I searched my memory I could not locate the date of my last visit, nor even the month in which it had occurred. I concluded that it had been less than a year. That was my best guess in any case.

After finding parking nearby I made my way to Pietro's. The parking ordeal took about 10 minutes of criss-crossing the grid of narrow streets that delineate the neighbourhood. I recalled that this was more or less the normal effort that had been required on past visits.

As I walked back up towards *via Tuscolana** I noted that the neighbourhood had not changed much during my self-imposed hiatus. This absence of change was somehow comforting to me in that moment. Predictably, that feeling did not stay with me for very long. It was enjoyable while it had lasted.

I was less than a block away when I saw it. The familiar sign, with the bright red background and yellow gold lettering was gone. In its place was an unrecognizable sign promoting a distinctly unfamiliar name.

My heart sank a little just then. I had been looking forward to this for

*See Glossary P. 203

over a week now. In fact, from the very moment I had found out that the business would finally take me to this part of town again, my anticipation had grown.

There was a time when the business took me to this neighbourhood Monday through Friday, each and every week. I worked out of an office on the same block as the *trattoria* and I used to have lunch at Pietro's once or twice a week for three years. A few of the folks in my office came here as well.

Over time, things changed. Not the restaurant, but the office did as colleagues drifted away to other adventures, myself included. Eventually, even the office itself moved on from the neighbourhood to the cheaper rents and ample free parking found in the suburbs.

They say that you can never step in the same river twice. I always went back to step in that river though. Whenever I had occasion to be in that part of town I went back. It has been nearly twenty years since I worked in the area, and yet here I am, still returning. Apparently, the others never went back and Pietro was a bit hurt by that. For what it is worth, I think that it was mostly because Anna-maria never came back to see him. She had been his favourite.

Each time that I visited Pietro always asked me, with a hopeful expression on his face, if I had news from Anna-maria. Each time I replied to him that I did not have any news from her as we were no longer in touch. When I told him, this he would break eye contact and look past me and out the window. It was as if he expected her to suddenly appear right at that moment. She never did. Eventually, he stopped asking me about her.

Anna-maria was a beautiful, kind and loving person who sparkled with life. She had such a playful and sensuous spirit, and so many generous talents. Yet there was, as I came to observe, a troubled darkness to her. In a sense she was tragically flawed. No crime there, as we are all flawed in our own ways. Upon reflection, I can't help but miss her. I knew that Pietro also missed her, but likely for very different reasons than mine.

I recalled with a smile the memory of her sharing with me how she cursed her partner for not arguing passionately with her like an Italian man should. I reminded her that he was a Canadian man and sarcastically suggested that she find herself an Italian man to fight with if that was a key ingredient of a relationship for her. She scowled at my logic and quickly changed the subject. That was classic Anna-maria!

On my sporadic visits over the past decade, I noted that it was only ever Pietro manning the joint. Back in the days when I was a regular, two plump sisters were usually there helping him with the lunch rush. Over time it seemed that the business had diminished. I had not seen the sisters there in years, and yet I did not want to pry into his affairs to find out why. There are some unseen lines that I am just not comfortable crossing. Besides, he seemed jovial enough each time that

I saw him.

Who knows what burdens are weighing upon people we are only superficially acquainted with on the basis of commerce? Probably their burdens are very similar to ours. Those burdens, our little struggles that we try so hard to keep hidden from the world as best that we can. Most people can see through that, and besides...nothing can remain hidden forever.

Whatever else may have been going on below the surface, I noted that Pietro's kitchen was spotless and well-choreographed, just as it always had been. Nothing was out of place, and tempting aromas were perpetually circulating. Based upon his appearance you would expect nothing less from Pietro: ramrod straight posture, meticulously groomed, and starched cook's whites crowned by a hipster fedora. Of course he had been wearing that fedora since well before there were hipsters. The fedora was the one asymmetrical element in the equation. Yet, in its own way it fit in perfectly...precisely because, at first glance, it did not seem to fit in.

All of these memories of Pietro and his *trattoria* came back to me as I tried to reconcile the meaning of the new sign. Maybe Pietro had finally hung up his apron and retired after years of six day work weeks? Wherever he is now, I will bet you that he is still wearing his fedora.

As I drew closer I could see that some of the inside signage was still the same and that gave me some hope. Still, the marquee sign was now advertising cakes and this made no sense at all. Pietro's had never had cakes on offer before. This was all very confusing to me, these contra indicators. I was now only steps away from getting some definitive answers. I hoped that these would eliminate my confusion.

They hit me immediately as I walked through the door! The familiar tempting aromas were dancing seductively in the air, just as they always had ever since my first visit. These aromas impacted me on a very visceral level as my senses kicked in and pushed my appetite to top priority status. I went along for this journey, just as I always had.

Gazing across the counter to the open kitchen, I could see the usual collection of gleaming pots on the stove top, seven or eight of them pumping out those tempting aromas. What I did not see was Pietro. I carefully scanned the place top to bottom again and still no Pietro.

One of the sisters was there. Patrizia was her name. At first I was not certain that it was her as I had not seen her in nearly twenty years. She did not recognize me. I asked her where Pietro was and she just smiled and asked me how I knew him.

I told her the story of how I was a regular years ago, of where I had worked, and then I mentioned Anna-maria. The moment that she heard Anna-maria's name her face lit up. Then a flicker of recognition came into her eyes, after she had studiously looked me over for a second time. Patrizia asked me if I had any news from Anna-maria, just as Pietro always did. I gave her the same answer that I always gave to him. She did not look out the window after my response as he typically had.

How did it come to pass that Anna-maria had made such a profound impression on these folks, and then simply vanished from their lives? Sadly, this is an all too common occurrence, and only in the minority of cases is it justifiably the result of extreme life circumstances. At the end of the day, the unfortunate truth is that someone always leaves. Interpersonal relationships have become a disposable commodity; another casualty of the instant gratification age.

What is the point of it all? Why cross over those unseen lines and start building something that will ultimately be abandoned? Left to wither and rot from one-sided neglect once the effort to maintain it becomes even a tad inconvenient? Today we are more connected than ever and yet we have drifted farther apart from each other in the ways that truly matter. The authentic is being regularly sacrificed for speed and convenience. Did Anna-maria ever think about Pietro or Patrizia? I would not have bet on it.

What I can share with you now is that Anna-maria lived in a different world from the rest of us. Her world was a place of beauty, art, passion, the past, culture, people and love. It was a world increasingly mired in a struggle for relevance, and time seemed to be running out. I am certain that she knew this, even though she would never admit it.

The inconvenient truth was that her world was disappearing

because it was not aligned with the unforgiving balance sheet oppression of our current era. No escape from economic marginalization, and the collateral damage of wealth inequality and political polarization that dominates our times. Welcome to the New World Order.

Her world was where she lived in the beauty of the moment; dogmatic in her belief that she and her world had all the time that they would ever need. I enjoyed the privilege of spending time with her there on the few occasions when she invited me to do so. I did not truly understand or appreciate it then, but in retrospect I do now.

She was very comfortable in the moment and accustomed to living day-to-day. I was not. I always had an eye gazing upon the future. I needed plans and to make progress towards them. She did not. We both thought that our respective paths were the ideal. It is only with the passing of some years that I can recognize my unwarranted fear of the pure simplicity of her chosen world. She was right, and I was wrong. It took me years to understand and accept that.

Patrizia asked me if I remembered her and her sister. I told her that I did. I asked her where she had been hiding for the past decade, and why she and her sister had left poor Pietro by himself to run the *trattoria*. She just smiled again, even wider this time. A glint of mischief sparkled in her eyes as she told me that she'd pop by '*once in a blue moon.*' I laughed and told that her that it had been the same for me. She asked me why and I explained to her about the business.

I asked her for my 'usual', and then teased her that she probably did not remember what it was. She didn't hesitate for a second: *"Spaghetti alle Vongole, with a little extra garlic."* she stated confidently.

"Esatamente, that is what I have been craving for nearly a year now." I replied. Thinking aloud, I mused that I really should make a greater effort to shorten the time intervals between my visits. Patrizia only chuckled in reply.

Life and work complicate things. All too often it seems that our time vanishes. Our good intentions are left unfulfilled, entries on a to-do list that never seem to get crossed off as completed. The ones that we do manage to get crossed off the list are soon forgotten. They are immediately replaced by three or four new entries that require our time and energies. That is the treadmill that is too often mistaken as being a meaningful life.

I took a seat near the window and waited on my meal. As I waited I looked out the window but was not really seeing anything. I was lost in thought now with the mystery of how *Time* disappears from us. Of how *Time* can so subtly fade into the background, over-shadowed by the complications of life as it gets tangled up in relationships, events and responsibilities...actual, imaginary, or manufactured complications.

Time never sleeps, and it never takes a day off. The value of *Time* must be acknowledged and respected. After all, even a broken clock is right twice a day. Consider the notion that *Time* is a form of currency.

Every day, we each get twenty-four hours of *Time* to spend as we choose.

However, it is an inescapable fact that *Time* eventually deserts each of us. One day we get less than twenty-four hours. *Time* moves on, as it must, and on that day it leaves us behind forever. On that day, there is no place under the sky for us to hide.

Have you ever wondered about people who wasted their time mired in trivialities and minutiae? I used to wonder about that. Later, I came to the recognition that they were caught up in their own journey. In the final analysis how could they possibly know what they did not know even existed? The simple answer was that they could not.

I was snapped back into the moment by a plate of *spaghetti alle vongole* being set down in front of me. Patrizia smiled warmly at me. I asked her again where Pietro was, and why they had changed the name of the *trattoria*. She was still smiling but a subtle flicker of sadness now appeared in her eyes. Gently she placed her hand on my arm as she said: *"Enjoy your meal now and we will speak about it when you are done."* She had her reasons and I respected that.

The pasta was good, but it was no longer Pietro's. Certainly its origins and pedigree were readily identifiable. It did have many of the subtle nuances characteristic of Pietro's art within it. Yet it was lacking in some way. Perhaps lacking is too harsh a word. Maybe a little different is a kinder way to describe it. Every chef has secrets. Their secrets are the DNA that make their creations uniquely theirs. That is their artistry and their mastery.

Once I had cleaned my plate, Patrizia approached with a bottle of *limoncello* and two small glasses. As the restaurant was empty, save for the two of us, she sat down with me and poured us each a shot. She raised her glass and gestured that I should follow suit. Pietro and I had done this many times in the past. This was my first occasion to do so with Patrizia.

"Brindisi, to Pietro." She said softly. We clinked our glasses together, and then reclaimed them so that we could each take a sip. In that precise moment, as I drew my glass back, I realized where Pietro was.

As I processed this knowledge I could feel waves of conflicting emotions rising up within me. Happiness and gratitude clashed with sadness and regret. These contrary pairings were trying to assert their dominance over each other. Why can't it be both at once? Not necessarily in equal measures, but co-existing on some level since each of them has validity and purpose.

"He passed peacefully in his sleep. He had not been sick. He went to bed as normal and... he just didn't wake up the next day." Patrizia told me as she held my hand. As I processed this information I simultaneously wondered if she was holding my hand to comfort me or herself. Probably both I decided. I let that observation go and shifted my focus back to the story that Patrizia was telling me.

The funeral had been a few months back and many customers had attended. Some had even given brief speeches highlighting their memories of the times that they had shared with Pietro in the *trattoria*. I placed my free hand over her hand, the one that held my other hand, and told her that I was very sorry not to have been there to say goodbye.

I could feel my eyes misting with emotions now, and so I turned my gaze from Patrizia to the window hoping that the world outside would distract me. The Universe provides; at that moment a customer walked into the *trattoria*. Patrizia gently withdrew her hand from mine, and went to seat him.

My attention briefly shifted from the world outside to the new arrival. He seemed vaguely familiar to me and yet I could not place him definitively. At that moment in time there was no way that I could have known that we would meet again only a few weeks from now. It would be at a different restaurant, near *Termini*, and owing to a simple twist of fate we would end up dining together. On that day, he would again seem vaguely familiar to me, yet I would not remember having seen him here today. I turned my gaze away from the Old Man and back out the window where I lost myself in thought.

Patrizia eventually rejoined me. Over an hour has passed since she had left, yet it seemed like only a few seconds to me. The *trattoria* was now empty, except for us. Patrizia took my hand again: *"You look sad."* she told me.

"Yes, of course I am a little sad. And that is OK." I replied.

As she picked up the bottle of *limoncello* and refilled our glasses Patrizia told me with a grin *"He was laid to rest in his cook's whites and his fedora."*

I could not help but smile at this vision that she had just planted on me. The natural order was aligned and Pietro's story had concluded exactly as it was meant to. As I raised my glass, I took her free hand in mine, gave it a squeeze and said: *"Brindisi! To our friend and brother Pietro!"*

The simple truth is that someone always leaves. It must be this way.

Glossary of Translations

Author's note

The Glossary of Translations is meant to provide the essential meaning and context for the respective words and expressions. The translations are not meant to be rigorously exact in the academic sense.

The phrase *'lost in translation'* comes to mind.

Glossary of Translations

Pastore Nero

Centro	Downtown
Linea A	Subway Line A
Metropolitana	Metro / Subway
Guilio Agricola	A suburban subway station
Pza. / Piazza	A plaza / A gathering place
Manzoni	A suburban subway station
Villa Borghese	A large park in Rome
Via Tuscolana	A major street in Rome
Vespa	An Italian Scooter Brand
Pastore Nero	The Black Shepherd
Acqueducto	Ancient Roman aqueduct
Ciampino	An airport in Rome
Cinecitta	A famous movie studio
Colli Albani	A suburban subway station
Furio Camillo	A suburban subway station

	Via Roma
Trattoria	A Small Restaurant

The Poetry of a Small Bird

Via Nardones	A street in Naples
Quartieri Spagnoli	A neighbourhood in Naples
Moka	A stovetop coffee maker
Doppio	Double (espresso coffee)

Trattoria no.2

Termini	Rome's main train station
La Dolce Vita	The Sweet Life
Antipasto	An appetizer
Primi	The first course of a meal
Nero d'Avola	A Sicilian red wine
Merci Monsieur	Thank you Sir
Vous parlez Francais	You speak French
Mais bien sur	But of course

Glossary of Translations

Fellini (Federico)	Famous Italian Director
la Republica	An Italian daily newspaper
la Scarpetta	The little shoe
Napoli	The City of Naples
Limoncello	A liqueur made of lemons
Campania	A Region in Southern Italy

The Gifts

Metropolitana	Metro / Subway
Centro	Downtown (Centre)
Guilio Agricola	A suburban subway station
Bodhisattva	One whose essence is enlightenment
Termini	Rome's main train station
Piazza Republica	A famous plaza in Rome
Via Alessandria	A street in Rome
Barista	A person who makes coffees

Via Roma

Gazetta de la Sport	A daily sports newspaper
Un café per favore	A coffee please
Macchina	A coffee machine
Amico	A Friend / Buddy
Americano	American
No Sono Americano	I am not an American
Sono Canadese	I am a Canadian
Faux-pas	a tactless act or speech
Molto Simpatico	Very nice / very pleasant
Amico Canadese	A Canadian friend
Italiano	Italian
Grazie	Thank you
A Presto	See you later
Sanpietrini	Cobblestones in Rome
Aspeta	Have patience
Furio Camillo	A suburban subway station

Glossary of Translations

Piazza / Pza.	A plaza / A gathering place
Peroni	An Italian beer company
Trattoria	A small restaurant
Sale e Pepe	Salt and Pepper (Hair)
Pince-nez	A style of reading glasses
Bucatini all'Amatriaciana	A spicy pasta dish
Teatro	The Theatre
Essattamente	Exactly / Precisely
Pancetta	A type of Italian bacon
Carravaggio	A famous Italian painter

The Room with no Door

Morpheus	Greek God of Sleep & Dreams
Palazzo	A Palace / Mansion
Ministerio	A Government Ministry
il Duce	The Duke (Mussolini)

Via Roma

Pza. Venezia	A famous plaza in Rome
Primavera	The Spring season
Acapella	Singing without instruments
Puccini	Italian composer (19th Century)
Nessum Dorma	Aria from Turandot (Puccini opera)
Capitolio	Capitol Building in Rome
Terrazzo	A Terrace

An Unexpected Virtue of Solitude (Some Always Leaves)

Pza. Garibaldi	A major plaza in Naples
Poquito	A little bit (Spanish)
Via Toledo	A major street in Naples
Teatro di San Carlo	A famous theatre in Naples
Galleria Umberto I	A vintage shopping mall in Naples
Assassino	An Assassin
Retrouvaille	A reunion, after a long seperation

Glossary of Translations

Pza. Plebiscito	A major plaza in Naples
Art Nouveau	Design style of the late 19th century
Belle Epoque	The comfortable period preceding WW I
Trattoria	A small restaurant

Last Swim in the Tiber

Tiber	Major river in Rome
Ponte San Angelo	San Angelo Bridge
Passegiatta	A stroll or a walk
Piazza de la Republica	A famous plaza in Rome
Fontana delle Naiadi	Rutelli's fountain in Pza. Republica
Rutelli (Mario)	An Italian sculptor
Piazza	A plaza / gathering place
Esquilino	A neighbourhood in Rome
Monti	A neighbourhood in Rome
San Lorenzo	A neighbourhood in Rome

Via Roma

Via Veneto	A famous street in Rome
Pincio	Scenic Outlook in Villa Borghese
Villa Borghese	Famous Villa and Park in Rome
Pza. del Poplo	A famous square in Rome
Piazza Navona	A famous square in Rome
Lungotevere Tor di Nona	A street in Rome
Trastevere	A neighbourhood in Rome
Ponte Gardibaldi	A bridge in Rome
Lungotevere di Cenci	A street in Rome
Testaccio	A neighbourhood in Rome
Tempus Fugit	Time Flies

Carnival Masks

Regionales	Regional Trains (Slow ones!)
Ventimiglia	A town on the Italian Riviera
Napoli	A city in the Campagnia region (South)

Glossary of Translations

Genoa	A city in the Liguria region (North west)
Livorno	A town in the Liguria region (North west)
Cinque Terre	A picturesque area in the Liguria region
Vernazza	A village in Cinque Terre
Piazza	A plaza / A gathering place
Almendrones	Cuban slang for old American cars
Rubicon	A river in north-eastern Italy

Someone Always Leaves – II & III

Campania	A Region in Southern Italy
Tiber	A Large River in Rome
Centro	The Downtown
Termini	Rome's main train station
Pincio	A scenic lookout in Rome
Lido	A beach, or outdoor swimming pool
Ostia	A district of Rome on the Tyrrhenian Sea

Tossing Coins

Primavera	The Spring season
Terra Firma	Solid Ground
Fiumicino	Rome's main airport
Centro	Downtown
Termini	Rome's Main Train Station
Kaizen	Perpetual incremental improvement
Lire	Italian coins (pre-dates Euro)
Bella Roma	Beautiful Rome
Trevi	Famous Fountain in Rome
La Dolce Vita	The Sweet Life (Famous Fellini Film)
Campo di Fiori	A famous piazza in Rome
Via del Corso	A major street in Rome

The Son She never Had

Sei Pazzo	You are crazy!

Glossary of Translations

La Famiglia	The Family
Sei Molto Pazzo	You are very crazy!
Andiamo	Let's Go!
Via Turatti	A street in Rome
Nostradamus	French Astrologer & Prophet
Basta	Enough already, Stop it!
Incorrigible	Incorrigible
Tavola	The dinner table
Trattoria	A small restaurant
Stranieri	A Stranger (Foreigner)
Complimenti	My Compliments
Mi Piace Molto	I Like it very much
La Cucina	The cuisine
Senti	Listen

Dinner with Ciro

Via Roma

Nonas	Grandmothers
Senti	Listen
Osteria	A Restaurant
Fontanelle	A neighbourhhod in Naples
Sanita	A neighbourhhod in Naples
Pizzaiolo	A chef who specializes in pizzas
Capello Nero per Due	Black Hat for Two
Trattoria	A Small Restaurant
Passegiatta	After Dinner Stroll
Quartieri Spagnoli	A neighbourhood in Naples
Vespa Gialla	A yellow Vespa scooter
Veni	Come on / Come here
Pasta e Fagioli	Pasta and Beans
Gelateria	An Ice Cream Shop
Napoli	A city in the Campagnia region (South)

Glossary of Translations

Someone Always Leaves – IV

Dolcezza	Sweetheart
Puccini	Italian composer (19th Century)
e respiro immaginifico	To be more than breathless
Le Grand Amour perdu	The great love lost (French)

Unusual Storms

Duomo	Famous Church in Milan
Milano Centrale	Milan's main train station
Trattoria	A small restaurant
Barista	A person who makes coffees
Avant-garde	Unusual or experimental ideas
Cappuccino	A style of coffee
Regionales	Regional trains
Partenze	Departures Board(Trains)
Ventimiglia	A coastal town in Italy
Binario	A railway track platform

Via Roma | A type of pastry

Brioche | A type of pastry

Someone Always Leaves – Coda

Via Tuscolana	A street in Rome
Trattoria	A small restaurant
Spaghetti alle Vongole	Spaghetti in clam sauce
Esatamente	Exactly, or Precisely
Limoncello	A liqueur made from lemons
Brindisi	Cheers, to your health
Termini	Rome's Main Train Station

Acknowledgments

I wish to offer massive gratitude to the following folks for their generosity and support in bringing this project to fruition.

You were universal in your encouragement. Some of you offered profound editorial insights, while others inspired me in subtle ways that shaped the direction of several of the stories. I am eternally grateful for the gifts that each of you generously gave to me.

Luca Bucaioni
Trish Campbell
Arfona Zwiers
Kathy Wolverton
Sieyf Shahabudeen

Photo: David L. Vaughan

Robert T. Norton

Via Roma is the Author's first book. It was inspired by over a dozen visits to la Bella Paese over the past three decades.

The Greater Toronto Area (GTA) is the Author's base camp for life, career and the creative pursuits of photography, writing, and painting. You can learn more with a visit to:

www.eyesonphoto.tours

CPSIA information can be obtained
at www.ICGtesting.com
Printed in the USA
BVHW041325020222
627784BV00014B/1245